IN THE BEGINNING . . .
OF THE END

The diver was still alive.

The Youngest could bring him to the cave quite easily. She hesitated, then extended her head toward the air tanks on his back, took the tanks in her jaws and began to carry him.

She brought him, still unconscious, to the ledge at the back of the cave and reared her head a good eight feet out of the water to lift him up on it. As she set him down softly on the bare rock, one of his legs brushed her neck. A thrill of icy horror split the warm interior of her body.

She had broken the taboo.

Suddenly she was terribly frightened, frightened that what she had done was irreparable . . . a signal marking the end of everything for them all!

Also edited by Judy-Lynn del Rey:

STELLAR #1
STELLAR SCIENCE FICTION STORIES #2

Published by Ballantine Books

Stellar
SHORT NOVELS

EDITED BY
Judy-Lynn del Rey

BALLANTINE BOOKS • NEW YORK

To Ron Busch,
the best damned publisher
an editor ever had,
and
to his delightful wife
Shelley

Library of Congress Catalog Card Number: 76-18081

ISBN 0-345-25501-1-150

Manufactured in the United States of America

First Edition: October 1976

Cover art by Darrell Sweet

Contents

INTRODUCTION:
An Endangered Species

This book had to be. There are stories in science fiction which cannot be told in a few words, and yet will not fill a book; stories, which, caught in the limbo between short stories and full-length novels, may flicker briefly in a magazine but are less likely to manage the permanence of book publication. And yet—they deserve to live.

History has a strange way of repeating itself. Those exact words were first written by Frederik Pohl in his introductory remarks to a book called *Star Short Novels*, which Ballantine published in 1954. Now they appear again, very appropriately, in the introduction to *Stellar Short Novels*. If those two titles seem remarkably similar, there's a reason; and that is only the first of several interesting coincidences.

Back in the early 1950's, Fred was editing a series of original anthologies—a rather novel idea for its time. *Star Science Fiction #1* and *Star Science Fiction #2* each featured a dozen-plus stories by the top names in the field: Asimov, Bradbury, Clarke, and the like. When Fred happened upon an sf novella by famed mainstream writer Jessamyn West, he decided to showcase the story in a volume consisting of three short novels. But first, he had to find the other two stories, which he eventually commissioned from Lester del Rey and Theodore Sturgeon—and, *voilà*: *Star Short Novels* was created.

Twenty years later I arrived at Ballantine, having served a lengthy apprenticeship under Frederik Pohl at *Galaxy Magazine** and was casting about for an apt title for—what else?—a series of original sf anthologies.

---

* But that's a story for another day . . . a story Fred will tell in his memoirs *The Way the Future Was* which he is currently finishing and which Ballantine will eventually publish. We have it on good authority that several people are poised to sue!

The marketplace was already cluttered with *Novas* and *Orbits* and *Universes* and other such cosmic concoctions. But since it seemed appropriate to try to pick up where Fred left off in 1959 with *Star #6,* I decided to launch *Son of Star* or, updated *Stellar #1.* It seemed like a good idea at the time, and *Stellar #2* quickly followed. Then —and here's where the coincidences really begin to get thick—Gordy Dickson turned up with a long novella that was too long for *Stellar #3* and much too good to let go elsewhere. So, what to do? Fortunately—or, maybe, miraculously—within a week, two more very long stories appeared out of nowhere. Then—as if demanded by tradition—*Stellar Short Novels* assembled itself before my eyes.

It remains to be seen whether history will come full circle and produce at least four more books in the series. Even as I write this, *Stellar #3* still needs another 30,000 words of fiction before it is a book ready to be published. Unfortunately, finding the additional stories may be easier said than done. In this, the age of the paperback novel, there are few incentives for sf writers to produce short fiction. Indeed the short story has become something of an endangered species. But where there's life there's hope, and in every mail more manuscripts continually materialize. And every editor can hope that another "Nightfall" or a new "Martian Odyssey" or even the next "Helen O'Loy" will be among them. The short story may be an endangered species, but at least it is not yet extinct.

Speaking of endangered species brings us to that lovely lady who adorns the front cover of this book: Nessie, the Loch Ness Monster and heroine of Gordy Dickson's lively story. Whether or not Nessie really exists (and I would like to believe she does) is still up in the air—or, more precisely, down in the depths of the Loch.

This fabled beast has been much in the news during the last year. In fact, her picture—or at least a fuzzy photo that some photographers claim is her picture— has even appeared on the front page of *The New York*

Times. That distinguished newspaper has dispatched a well-financed expedition to Loch Ness to determine once and for all if there is more substance than shadow to that marvelous myth. And suppose there is, then what? Once Nessie surfaces, she—and any members of her family who might come to light with her—instantly become one of the endangered species of the world and creatures to be protected and respected.

How we humans relate to Nessie will tell us an awful lot about ourselves and about how we might react should we ever be presented with a representative of an extra-terrestrial race. If first impressions are any indication of what is to come, then we humans are in big trouble. When I was in England in November 1975, the pictures mentioned above were just being leaked to the press. Sure enough the bold headline on the front page of the Sunday paper said: NESSIE REARS HER UGLY HEAD! On behalf of Loch Ness Monsters everywhere, I took instant umbrage. What did Nessie ever do to deserve that? She's never hurt anybody, never caused anyone the slightest trouble. And what makes her ugly? Different, maybe; but ugly? Surely not to another Loch Ness Monster.

The situation was not much better when I came home to New York and read about the "revolting monster" that was about to make her debut. If this journalistic xenophobia says anything about how Nessie will be treated if found, it is divinely to be wished that she stays where she is—undiscovered, undisturbed, and unharmed.

So much for the characters found in this book. Now a word about the authors who are also characters, but of a different sort.

Gordon R. Dickson, the Minneapolis Miracle, is a for-mer President of the Science Fiction Writers of America. Gordy also had a story in *Stellar #1* about a little girl whose grandfather was a tree. And this month Ballan-tine is publishing his new fantasy novel *The Dragon and the George.* It's an old-fashioned romp about a girl whose boyfriend is a dragon and the problems that en-sue. The book is available now, and it is a chuckle.

Andrew J. Offutt (or andrew j. offutt, as he signs his

letters) is the current President of the Science Fiction Writers of America. He's written an sf/detective story for this book, and "The Greenhouse Defect" is a winner. But don't believe me, I'm prejudiced. Read the story and see if you don't agree. Andy has just sent in a sword-and-planet epic called *My Lord Barbarian,* which is full of swash and buckle and which we will publish early in 1977.

Richard S. Weinstein is not now nor has he ever been a President of the SFWA. But that's understandable since "Oceans Away" is his very first story. But stay tuned . . . Richard's presidential status may change by next year, at which time his first novel should be finished.

In this year of America's bicentennial and the quincentennial celebrated in Arthur C. Clarke's *Imperial Earth,* it is only proper to wish science fiction—as we know it, as a category—a very happy fiftieth birthday. All of us involved in science fiction in one way or another—as readers, as writers, as editors, as publishers—owe a great deal to Hugo Gernsback and to that first issue of *Amazing Stories:* April 1926. And while we're about it, here's to the hundredth anniversary of that same event, with the hope that science fiction will be as prosperous in 2076 as it is in 1976 . . . and that a lot of you will be around to celebrate!

—Judy-Lynn del Rey
New York, New York
July 4, 1976

The Mortal and the Monster

Gordon R. Dickson

That summer more activity took place upon the shores of the loch and more boats appeared on its waters than at any time in memory. Among them was even one of the sort of boats that went underwater. It moved around in the loch slowly, diving quite deep at times. From the boats, swimmers with various gear about them descended on lines—but not so deep—swam around blindly for a while, and then returned to the surface.

Brought word of all this in her cave, First Mother worried and speculated on disaster. First Uncle, though equally concerned, was less fearful. He pointed out that the Family had survived here for thousands of years; and that it could not all end in a single year—or a single day.

Indeed, the warm months of summer passed one by one with no real disturbance to their way of life.

Suddenly fall came. One night, the first snow filled the air briefly above the loch. The Youngest danced on the surface in the darkness, sticking out her tongue to taste the cold flakes. Then the snow ceased, the sky cleared for an hour, and the banks could be seen gleaming white under a high and watery moon. But the clouds covered the moon again; and because of the relative

1

warmth of the loch water nearby, in the morning, when the sun rose, the shores were once more green.

With dawn, boats began coming and going on the loch again and the Family went deep, out of sight. In spite of this precaution, trouble struck from one of these craft shortly before noon. First Uncle was warming the eggs on the loch bottom in the hatchhole, a neatly cleaned shallow depression scooped out by Second Mother, near Glen Urquhart, when something heavy and round descended on a long line, landing just outside the hole and raising an almost-invisible puff of silt in the blackness of the deep, icy water. The line tightened and began to drag the heavy thing about.

First Uncle had his huge length coiled about the clutch of eggs, making a dome of his body and enclosing them between the smooth skin of his underside and the cleaned lakebed. Fresh, hot blood pulsed to the undersurface of his smooth skin, keeping the water warm in the enclosed area. He dared not leave the clutch to chill in the cold loch, so he sent a furious signal for Second Mother, who, hearing that her eggs were in danger, came swiftly from her feeding. The Youngest heard also and swam up as fast as she could in mingled alarm and excitement.

She reached the hatchhole just in time to find Second Mother coiling herself around the eggs, her belly skin already beginning to radiate heat from the warm blood that was being shunted to its surface. Released from his duties, First Uncle shot up through the dark, peaty water like a sixty-foot missile, up along the hanging line, with the Youngest close behind him.

They could see nothing for more than a few feet because of the murkiness. But neither First Uncle nor the Youngest relied much on the sense of sight, which was used primarily for protection on the surface of the loch, in any case. Besides, First Uncle was already beginning to lose his vision with age, so he seldom went to the surface nowadays, preferring to do his breathing in the caves, where it was safer. The Youngest had asked him once if he did not miss the sunlight, even the misty and often cloud-dulled sunlight of the open sky over the loch, with its instinctive pull at ancestral memories of the ocean, retold in the legends. No, he had told her, he had grown beyond such things. But she found it hard to believe him; for in her, the yearning for the mysterious and fascinating world above the waters was still strong. The Family had no word for it. If they did, they might have called her a romantic.

Now, through the pressure-sensitive cells in the cheek areas of her narrow head, she picked up the movements of a creature no more than six feet in length. Carrying some long, narrow made thing, the intruder was above them, though descending rapidly, parallel to the line.

"Stay back," First Uncle signaled her sharply; and, suddenly fearful, she lagged behind. From the vibrations she felt, their visitor could only be one of the upright animals from the world above that walked about on its hind legs and used "made" things. There was an ancient taboo about touching one of these creatures.

The Youngest hung back, then, continuing to rise through the water at a more normal pace.

Above her, through her cheek cells, she felt and interpreted the turbulence that came from First Uncle's movements. He flashed up, level with the descending animal, and with one swirl of his massive body snapped the taut descending line. The animal was sent tumbling— untouched by First Uncle's bulk (according to the taboo), but stunned and buffeted and thrust aside by the water-blow like a leaf in a sudden gust of wind when autumn sends the dry tears of the trees drifting down upon the shore waters of the loch.

The thing the animal had carried, as well as the lower half of the broken line, began to sink to the bottom. The top of the line trailed aimlessly. Soon the upright animal, hanging limp in the water, was drifting rapidly away from it. First Uncle, satisfied that he had protected the location of the hatchhole for the moment, at least—though later in the day they would move the eggs to a new location, anyway, as a safety precaution—turned and headed back down to release Second Mother once more to her feeding.

Still fearful, but fascinated by the drifting figure, the Youngest rose timidly through the water on an angle that gradually brought her close to it. She extended her small head on its long, graceful neck to feel about it from close range with her pressure-sensitive cheek cells. Here, within inches of the floating form, she could read minute differences, even in its surface textures. It seemed to be encased in an unnatural outer skin—one of those skins the creatures wore which were not actually theirs—made of some material that soaked up the loch water. This soaked-up water was evidently heated by the interior temperature of the creature, much as members of the Family could warm their belly skins with shunted blood, which protected the animal's body inside by cutting down the otherwise too-rapid radiation of its heat into the cold liquid of the loch.

The Youngest noticed something bulky and hard on the creature's head, in front, where the eyes and mouth were. Attached to the back was a larger, doubled something, also hard and almost a third as long as the creature itself. The Youngest had never before seen a diver's wetsuit, swim mask, and air tanks with pressure regulator, but she had heard them described by her elders. First Mother had once watched from a safe distance while a creature so equipped had maneuvered below the surface of the loch, and she had concluded that the things he wore were devices to enable him to swim underwater without breathing as often as his kind seemed to need to, ordinarily.

Only this one was not swimming. He was drifting away with an underwater current of the loch, rising slowly as he traveled toward its south end. If he continued like this, he would come to the surface near the center of the loch. By that time the afternoon would be over. It would be dark.

Clearly, he had been damaged. The blow of the water

that had been slammed at him by the body of First Uncle had hurt him in some way. But he was still alive. The Youngest knew this, because she could feel through her cheek cells the slowed beating of his heart and the movement of gases and fluids in his body. Occasionally, a small thread of bubbles came from his head to drift surfaceward.

It was a puzzle to her where he carried such a reservoir of air. She herself could contain enough oxygen for six hours without breathing, but only a portion of that was in gaseous form in her lungs. Most was held in pure form, saturating special tissues throughout her body.

Nonetheless, for the moment the creature seemed to have more than enough air stored about him; and he still lived. However, it could not be good for him to be drifting like this into the open loch with night coming on. Particularly if he was hurt, he would be needing some place safe out in the air, just as members of the Family did when they were old or sick. These upright creatures, the Youngest knew, were slow and feeble swimmers. Not one of them could have fed himself, as she did, by chasing and catching the fish of the loch; and very often when one fell into the water at any distance from the shore, he would struggle only a little while and then die.

This one would die also, in spite of the things fastened to him, if he stayed in the water. The thought raised a sadness in her. There was so much death. In any century, out of perhaps five clutches of a dozen eggs to a clutch, only one embryo might live to hatch. The legends claimed that once, when the Family had lived in the sea, matters had been different. But now, one survivor out of several clutches was the most to be hoped for. A hatchling who survived would be just about the size of this creature, the Youngest thought, though of course not with his funny shape. Nevertheless, watching him was a little like watching a new hatchling, knowing it would die.

It was an unhappy thought. But there was nothing to

be done. Even if the diver were on the surface now, the chances were small that his own People could locate him.

Struck by a thought, the Youngest went up to look around. The situation was as she had guessed. No boats were close by. The nearest was the one from which the diver had descended; but it was still anchored close to the location of the hatchhole, nearly half a mile from where she and the creature now were.

Clearly, those still aboard thought to find him near where they had lost him. The Youngest went back down, and found him still drifting, now not more than thirty feet below the surface, but rising only gradually.

Her emotions stirred as she looked at him. He was not a cold life-form like the salmons, eels, and other fishes on which the Family fed. He was warm—as she was—and if the legends were all true, there had been a time and a place on the wide oceans where one of his ancestors and one of her ancestors might have looked at each other, equal and unafraid, in the open air and the sunlight.

So, it seemed wrong to let him just drift and die like this. He had shown the courage to go down into the depths of the loch, this small, frail thing. And such courage required some recognition from one of the Family, like herself. After all, it was loyalty and courage that had kept the Family going all these centuries: their loyalty to each other and the courage to conserve their strength and go on, hoping that someday the ice would come once more, the land would sink, and they would be set free into the seas again. Then surviving hatchlings would once more be numerous, and the Family would begin to grow again into what the legends had once called them, a "True People." Anyone who believed in loyalty and courage, the Youngest told herself, ought to respect those qualities wherever she found them—even in one of the upright creatures.

He should not simply be left to die. It was a daring thought, that she might interfere . . .

She felt her own heart beating more rapidly as she followed him through the water, her cheek cells only inches from his dangling shape. After all, there was the taboo. But perhaps, if she could somehow help him without actually touching him . . . ?

"Him," of course, should not include the "made" things about him. But even if she could move him by these made parts alone, where could she take him?

Back to where the others of his kind still searched for him?

No, that was not only a deliberate flouting of the taboo but was very dangerous. Behind the taboo was the command to avoid letting any of his kind know about the Family. To take him back was to deliberately risk that kind of exposure for her People. She would die before doing that. The Family had existed all these centuries only because each member of it was faithful to the legends, to the duties, and to the taboos.

But, after all, she thought, it wasn't that she was actually going to break the taboo. She was only going to do something that went around the edge of it, because the diver had shown courage and because it was not his fault that he had happened to drop his heavy thing right beside the hatchhole. If he had dropped it anyplace else in the loch, he could have gone up and down its cable all summer and the Family members would merely have avoided that area.

What he needed, she decided, was a place out of the water where he could recover. She could take him to one of the banks of the loch. She rose to the surface again and looked around.

What she saw made her hesitate. In the darkening afternoon, the headlights of the cars moving up and down the roadways on each side of the loch were still visible in unusual numbers. From Fort Augustus at the south end of the loch to Castle Ness at the north, she saw more headlights about than ever before at this time of year, especially congregating by St. Ninian's, where the diver's boat was docked, nights.

No, it was too risky, trying to take him ashore. But she knew of a cave, too small by Family standards for any of the older adults, south of Urquhart Castle. The diver had gone down over the hatchhole, which had been constructed by Second Mother in the mouth of Urquhart Glen, close by St. Ninian's; and he had been drifting south ever since. Now he was below Castle Urquhart and almost level with the cave. It was a good, small cave for an animal his size, with ledge of rock that was dry above the water at this time of year; and during the day even a little light would filter through cracks where tree roots from above had penetrated its rocky roof.

The Youngest could bring him there quite easily. She hesitated again, but then extended her head toward the air tanks on his back, took the tanks in her jaws, and began to carry him in the direction of the cave.

As she had expected, it was empty. This late in the day there was no light inside; but since, underwater, her cheek cells reported accurately on conditions about her and, above water, she had her memory, which was ultimately reliable, she brought him—still unconscious—to the ledge at the back of the cave and reared her head a good eight feet out of the water to lift him up on it. As she set him down softly on the bare rock, one of his legs brushed her neck, and a thrill of icy horror ran through the warm interior of her body.

Now she had done it! She had broken the taboo. Panic seized her.

She turned and plunged back into the water, out through the entrance to the cave and into the open loch. The taboo had never been broken before, as far as she knew—never. Suddenly she was terribly frightened. She headed at top speed for the hatchhole. All she wanted was to find Second Mother, or the Uncle, or anyone, and confess what she had done, so that they could tell her that the situation was not irreparable, not a signal marking an end of everything for them all.

Halfway to the hatchhole, however, she woke to the

fact that it had already been abandoned. She turned immediately and began to range the loch bottom southward, her instinct and training counseling her that First Uncle and Second Mother would have gone in that direction, south toward Inverfarigaig, to set up a new hatchhole.

As she swam, however, her panic began to lessen and guilt moved in to take its place. How could she tell them? She almost wept inside herself. Here it was not many months ago that they had talked about how she was beginning to look and think like an adult; and she had behaved as thoughtlessly as if she was still the near-hatchling she had been thirty years ago.

Level with Castle Kitchie, she sensed the new location and homed in on it, finding it already set up off the mouth of the stream which flowed past that castle into the loch. The bed of the loch about the new hatchhole had been neatly swept and the saucer-shaped depression dug, in which Second Mother now lay warming the eggs. First Uncle was close by enough to feel the Youngest arrive, and he swept in to speak to her as she halted above Second Mother.

"Where did you go after I broke the line?" he demanded before she herself could signal.

"I wanted to see what would happen to the diver," she signaled back. "Did you need me? I would have come back, but you and Second Mother were both there."

"We had to move right away," Second Mother signaled. She was agitated. "It was frightening!"

"They dropped another line," First Uncle said, "with a thing on it that they pulled back and forth as if to find the first one they dropped. I thought it not wise to break a second one. One break could be a chance happening. Two, and even small animals might wonder."

"But we couldn't keep the hole there with that thing dragging back and forth near the eggs," explained Second Mother. "So we took them and moved without waiting to make the new hole here, first. The Uncle and

I carried them, searching as we went. If you'd been here, you could have held half of them while I made the hole by myself, the way I wanted it. But you weren't. We would have sent for First Mother to come from her cave and help us, but neither one of us wanted to risk carrying the eggs about so much. So we had to work together here while still holding the eggs."

"Forgive me," said the Youngest. She wished she were dead.

"You're young," said Second Mother. "Next time you'll be wiser. But you do know that one of the earliest legends says the eggs should be moved only with the utmost care until hatching time; and you know we think that may be one reason so few hatch."

"If none hatch now," said First Uncle to the Youngest, less forgiving than Second Mother, even though they were not his eggs, "you'll remember this and consider that maybe you're to blame."

"Yes," mourned the Youngest.

She had a sudden, frightening vision of this one and all Second Mother's future clutches failing to hatch and she herself proving unable to lay when her time came. It was almost unheard of that a female of the Family should be barren, but a legend said that such a thing did occasionally happen. In her mind's eye she held a terrible picture of First Mother long dead, First Uncle and Second Mother grown old and feeble, unable to stir out of their caves, and she herself—the last of her line—dying alone, with no one to curl about her to warm or comfort her.

She had intended, when she caught up with the other two members of the Family, to tell them everything about what she had done with the diver. But she could not bring herself to it now. Her confession stuck in her mind. If it turned out that the clutch had been harmed by her inattention while she had actually been breaking the taboo with one of the very animals who had threatened the clutch in the first place . . .

She should have considered more carefully. But, of

course, she was still too ignorant and irresponsible. First Uncle and Second Mother were the wise ones. First Mother, also, of course; but she was now too old to see a clutch of eggs through to hatching stage by herself alone, or with just the help of someone presently as callow and untrustworthy as the Youngest.

"Can I— It's dark now," she signaled. "Can I go feed, now? Is it all right to go?"

"Of course," said Second Mother, who switched her signaling to First Uncle. "You're too hard sometimes. She's still only half grown."

The Youngest felt even worse, intercepting that. She slunk off through the underwater, wishing something terrible could happen to her so that when the older ones did find out what she had done they would feel pity for her, instead of hating her. For a while she played with mental images of what this might involve. One of the boats on the surface could get her tangled in their lines in such a way that she could not get free. Then they would tow her to shore, and since she was so tangled in the line she could not get up to the surface, and since she had not breathed for many hours, she would drown on the way. Or perhaps the boat that could go underwater would find her and start chasing her and turn out to be much faster than any of them had ever suspected. It might even catch her and ram her and kill her.

By the time she had run through a number of these dark scenarios, she had begun almost automatically to hunt, for the time was in fact well past her usual second feeding period and she was hungry. As she realized this, her hunt became serious. Gradually she filled herself with salmon; and as she did so, she began to feel better. For all her bulk, she was swifter than any fish in the loch. The wide swim-paddle at the end of each of her four limbs could turn her instantly; and with her long neck and relatively small head outstretched, the streamlining of even her twenty-eight-foot body parted the waters she displaced with an absolute minimum of resistance. Last, and most important of all, was the great engine of her enormously powerful, lashing tail: that was the real drive behind her ability to flash above the loch bottom at speeds of up to fifty knots.

She was, in fact, beautifully designed to lead the life she led, designed by evolution over the generations from that early land-dwelling, omnivorous early mammal that was her ancestor. Actually, she was herself a member of the mammalian sub-class prototheria, a large and distant cousin of monotremes like the platypus and the echidna. Her cretaceous forebears had drifted over and become practicing carnivores in the process of readapting to life in the sea.

She did not know this herself, of course. The legends of the Family were incredibly ancient, passed down by the letter-perfect memories of the individual generations; but they actually were not true memories of what had been, but merely deductions about the past gradually evolved as her People had acquired communication and intelligence. In many ways, the Youngest was very like a human savage: a member of a Stone Age tribe where elaborate ritual and custom directed every action of her life except for a small area of individual freedom. And in that area of individual freedom she was as prone to ignorance and misjudgments about the world beyond the waters of her loch as any Stone Age human primitive was in dealing with the technological world beyond his familiar few square miles of jungle.

Because of this—and because she was young and healthy—by the time she had filled herself with salmon, the exercise of hunting her dinner had burned off a good deal of her feelings of shame and guilt. She saw, or thought she saw, more clearly that her real fault was in not staying close to the hatchhole after the first incident. The diver's leg touching her neck had been entirely accidental; and besides, the diver had been unconscious and unaware of her presence at that time. So no harm could have been done. Essentially, the taboo was still unbroken. But she must learn to stay on guard as the adults did, to anticipate additional trouble, once some had put in an appearance, and to hold herself ready at all times.

She resolved to do so. She made a solemn promise to herself not to forget the hatchhole again—ever.

Her stomach was full. Emboldened by the freedom of the night-empty waters above, for the loch was always clear of boats after sundown, she swam to the surface, emerging only a couple of hundred yards from shore. Lying there, she watched the unusual number of lights from cars still driving on the roads that skirted the loch.

But suddenly her attention was distracted from them. The clouds overhead had evidently cleared, some time since. Now it was a clear, frosty night and more than half the sky was glowing and melting with the northern lights. She floated, watching them. So beautiful, she thought, so beautiful. Her mind evoked pictures of all the Family who must have lain and watched the lights like this since time began, drifting in the arctic seas or resting on some skerry or ocean rock where only birds walked. The desire to see all the wide skies and seas of all the world swept over her like a physical hunger.

It was no use, however. The mountains had risen and they held the Family here, now. Blocked off from its primary dream, her hunger for adventure turned to a more possible goal. The temptation came to go and investigate the loch-going "made" things from which her diver had descended.

She found herself up near Dores, but she turned and went back down opposite St. Ninian's. The dock to which this particular boat was customarily moored was actually a mile below the village and had no illumination. But the boat had a cabin on its deck, amidships, and through the square windows lights now glowed. Their glow was different from that of the lights shown by the cars. The Youngest noted this difference without being able to account for it, not understanding that the headlights she had been watching were electric, but the illumination she now saw shining out of the cabin windows of the large, flat-hulled boat before her came from gas lanterns. She heard sounds coming from inside the cabin.

Curious, the Youngest approached the boat from the darkness of the lake, her head now lifted a good six feet out of the water so that she could look over the side railing. Two large, awkward-looking shapes rested on the broad deck in front of the cabin—one just in front, the other right up in the bow with its far end overhanging the water. Four more shapes, like the one in the bow but smaller, were spaced along the sides of the foredeck, two to a side. The Youngest slid through the little waves until she was barely a couple of dozen feet from the side of the boat. At that moment, two men came out of the cabin, strode onto the deck, and stopped by the shape just in front of the cabin.

The Youngest, though she knew she could not be seen against the dark expanse of the loch, instinctively sank down until only her head was above water. The two men stood, almost overhead, and spoke to each other.

Their voices had a strangely slow, sonorous ring to the ears of Youngest, who was used to hearing sound waves traveling through the water at four times the speed they moved in air. She did understand, of course, that they were engaged in meaningful communication, much as she and the others of the Family were when they signaled to each other. This much her People had learned about the upright animals: they communicated by making sounds. A few of these sounds—the *"Ness"* sound, which, like the other sound, *"loch,"* seemed to refer to the water in which the Family lived—were by now familiar. But she recognized no such noises among those made by the two above her; in fact, it would have been surprising if she had, for while the language was the one she was used to hearing, the accent of one of the two was Caribbean English, different enough from that of those living in the vicinity of the loch to make what she heard completely unintelligible.

". . . poor bastard," the other voice said.

"Man, you forget that 'poor bastard' talk, I tell you! He knew what he doing when he go down that line. He know what a temperature like that mean. A reading like that big enough for a blue whale. He just want the glory—he all alone swimming down with a speargun to drug that great beast. It the newspaper head-lines, man; that's what he after!"

"Gives me the creeps, anyway. Think we'll ever fish up the sensor head?"

"You kidding. Lucky we find *him*. No, we use the spare, like I say, starting early tomorrow. And I mean it, early!"

"I don't like it. I tell you, he's got to have relatives who'll want to know why we didn't stop after we lost him. It's his boat. It's his equipment. They'll ask who gave us permission to go on spending money they got coming, with him dead."

"You pay me some heed. We've got to try to find him, that's only right. We use the equipment we got—what else we got to use? Never mind his rich relatives. They just like him. He don't never give no damn for you or me or what it cost him, this expedition. He was born with money and all he want to do is write the book about how he an adventurer. We know what we hunt be down there, now. We capture it, then everybody happy. And you and me, we get what's in the contract, the five thousand extra apiece for taking it. Otherwise we don't get nothing—you back to that machine shop, me to the whaling, with the pockets empty. We out in the cold then, you recall that!"

"All right."

"You damn right, it all right. Starting tomorrow sun-up."

"I said *all right!*" The voice paused for a second be-fore going on. "But I'm telling you one thing. If we run into it, you better get it fast with a drug spear; because I'm not waiting. If I see it, I'm getting on the harpoon gun."

The other voice laughed.

"That's why he never let you near the gun when we

out before. But I don't care. Contract, it say alive or dead
we get what he promise us. Come on now, up the inn and
have us food and drink."

"I want a drink! Christ, this water's empty after
dark, with that law about no fishing after sundown. Anything could be out there!"

"Anything is. Come on, mon."

The Youngest heard the sound of their footsteps
backing off the boat and moving away down the dock
until they became inaudible within the night of the land.

Left alone, she lifted her head gradually out of the
water once more and cautiously examined everything
before her: big boat and small ones nearby, dock and
shore. There was no sound or other indication of anything living. Slowly, she once more approached the craft
the two had just left and craned her neck over its side.

The large shape in front of the cabin was box-like
like the boat, but smaller and without any apertures in
it. Its top sloped from the side facing the bow of the
craft to the opposite side. On that sloping face she saw
circles of some material that, although as hard as the
rest of the object, still had a subtly different texture
when she pressed her cheek cells directly against them.
Farther down from these, which were in fact the glass
faces of meters, was a raised plate with grooves in it.
The Youngest would not have understood what the
grooves meant, even if she had had enough light to see
them plainly; and even if their sense could have been
translated to her, the words "caloric sensor" would have
meant nothing to her.

A few seconds later, she was, however, puzzled to
discover on the deck beside this object another shape
which her memory insisted was an exact duplicate of
the heavy round thing that had been dropped to the
loch bed beside the old hatchhole. She felt all over it
carefully with her cheek cells, but discovered nothing
beyond the dimensions of its almost plumb-bob shape
and the fact that a line was attached to it in the same
way a line had been attached to the other. In this case,

the line was one end of a heavy coil that had a farther end connected to the box-like shape with the sloping top.

Baffled by this discovery, the Youngest moved forward to examine the strange object in the bow of the boat with its end overhanging the water. This one had a shape that was hard to understand. It was more complex, made up of a number of smaller shapes both round and boxy. Essentially, however, it looked like a mound with something long and narrow set on top of it, such as a piece of waterlogged tree from which the limbs had long since dropped off. The four smaller things like it, spaced two on each side of the foredeck, were not quite like the big one, but they were enough alike so that she ignored them in favor of examining the large one. Feeling around the end of the object that extended over the bow of the boat and hovered above the water, the Youngest discovered the log shape rotated at a touch and even tilted up and down with the mound beneath it as a balance point. On further investigation, she found that the log shape was hollow at the water end and was projecting beyond the hooks the animals often let down into the water with little dead fish or other things attached, to try to catch the larger fish of the loch. This end, however, was attached not to a curved length of metal, but to a straight metal rod lying loosely in the hollow log space. To the rod part, behind the barbed head, was joined the end of another heavy coil of line wound about a round thing on the deck. This line was much thicker than the one attached to the box with the sloping top. Experimentally, she tested it with her teeth. It gave—but did not cut when she closed her jaws on it—then sprang back, apparently unharmed, when she let it go.

All very interesting, but puzzling—as well it might be. A harpoon gun and spearguns with heads designed to inject a powerful tranquilizing drug on impact were completely outside the reasonable dimensions of the world as the Youngest knew it. The heat-sensing equipment that had been used to locate First Uncle's huge body as it lay on the loch bed warming the eggs was closer to being something she could understand. She and the rest of the Family used heat sensing themselves to locate and identify one another, though their natural abilities were nowhere near as sensitive as those of the instrument she had examined on the foredeck. At any rate, for now, she merely dismissed from her mind the question of what these things were. Perhaps, she thought, the upright animals simply liked to have odd shapes of "made" things around them. That notion reminded her of her diver; and she felt a sudden, deep curiosity about him, a desire to see if he had yet recovered and found his way out of the cave to shore.

She backed off from the dock and turned toward the south end of the loch, not specifically heading for the cave where she had left him but traveling in that general direction and turning over in her head the idea that perhaps she might take one more look at the cave. But she would not be drawn into the same sort of irresponsibility she had fallen prey to earlier in the day, when she had taken him to the cave! Not twice would she concern herself with one of the animals when she was needed by others of the Family. She decided, instead, to go check on Second Mother and the new hatchhole.

When she got to the hole, however, she found that Second Mother had no present need of her. The older female, tired from the exacting events of the day and heavy from feeding later than her usual time—for she had been too nervous, at first, to leave the eggs in First Uncle's care and so had not finished her feeding period until well after dark—was half asleep. She only untucked her head from the coil she had made of her body around and above the eggs long enough to make sure that the Youngest had not brought warning of some new threat. Reassured, she coiled up tightly again about the clutch and closed her eyes.

The Youngest gazed at her with a touch of envy. It must be a nice feeling, she thought, to shut out everything but yourself and your eggs. There was plainly nothing that Youngest was wanted for, here—and she had never felt less like sleeping herself. The night was full of mysteries and excitements. She headed once more north, up the lake.

She had not deliberately picked a direction, but suddenly she realized that unconsciously she was once more heading toward the cave where she had left the diver. She felt a strange sense of freedom. Second Mother was sleeping with her eggs. First Uncle by this time would have his heavy bulk curled up in his favorite cave and his head on its long neck resting on a ledge at the water's edge, so that he had the best of both the worlds of air and loch at the same time. The Youngest had the loch to herself, with neither Family nor animals to worry about. It was all hers, from Fort Augustus clear to Castle Ness.

The thought gave her a sense of power. Abruptly, she decided that there was no reason at all why she should not go see what had happened to the diver. She turned directly toward the cave, putting on speed.

At the last moment, however, she decided to enter the cave quietly. If he was really recovered and alert, she might want to leave again without being noticed. Like a cloud shadow moving silently across the surface of the waves, she slid through the underwater entrance of the cave, invisible in the blackness, her cheek cells reassuring her that there was no moving body in the water inside.

Once within, she paused again to check for heat radiation that would betray a living body in the water even if it was being held perfectly still. But she felt no heat. Satisfied, she lifted her head silently from the water inside the cave and approached the rock ledge where she had left him.

Her hearing told that he was still here, though her eyes were as useless in this total darkness as his must be. Gradually, that same, sensitive hearing filled in the image of his presence for her.

He still lay on the ledge, apparently on his side. She could hear the almost rhythmic scraping of a sort of metal clip he wore on the right side of his belt. It was scratching against the rock as he made steady, small movements. He must have come to enough to take off his head-things and back-things, however, for she heard no scraping from these. His breathing was rapid and hoarse, almost a panting. Slowly, sound by sound, she built up a picture of him, there in the dark. He was curled up in a tight ball, shivering.

The understanding that he was lying, trembling from the cold, struck the Youngest in her most vulnerable area. Like all the Family, she had vivid memories of what it had been like to be a hatchling. As eggs, the clutch was kept in open water with as high an oxygen content as possible until the moment for hatching came close. Then they were swiftly transported to one of the caves so that they would emerge from their shell into the land and air environment that their warm-blooded, air-breathing ancestry required. And a hatchling could not drown on a cave ledge. But, although he or she was protected there from the water, a hatchling was still vulnerable to the cold; and the caves were no warmer than the water—which was snow-fed from the mountains most of the year. Furthermore, the hatchling would not develop the layers of blubber-like fat that insulated an adult of the Family for several years. The life of someone like the Youngest began with the sharp sensations of cold as a newborn, and ended the same way, when aged body processes were no longer able to generate enough interior heat to keep the great hulk going. The first instinct of the hatchling was to huddle close to the warm belly skin of the adult on guard. And the first instinct of the adult was to warm the small, new life.

She stood in the shallow water of the cave, irresolute. The taboo, and everything that she had ever known, argued fiercely in her against any contact with the upright animal. But this one had already made a breach in her cosmos, had already been promoted from an "it" to a "he" in her thoughts; and her instincts cried out as strongly as her teachings, against letting him chill there on the cold stone ledge when she had within her the heat to warm him.

It was a short, hard, internal struggle; but her instincts won. After all, she rationalized, it was she who had brought him here to tremble in the cold. The fact that by doing so she had saved his life was beside the point.

Completely hidden in the psychological machinery that moved her toward him now was the lack in her life that was the result of being the last, solitary child of her kind. From the moment of hatching on, she had never had a playmate, never known anyone with whom she could share the adventures of growing up. An unconscious part of her was desperately hungry for a friend, a toy, anything that could be completely and exclusively hers, apart from the adult world that encompassed everything around her.

Slowly, silently, she slipped out of the water and up onto the ledge and flowed around his shaking form. She did not quite dare to touch him; but she built walls about him and a roof over him out of her body, the inward-facing skin of which was already beginning to pulse with hot blood pumped from deep within her.

Either dulled by his semi-consciousness or else too wrapped up in his own misery to notice, the creature showed no awareness that she was there. Not until the warmth began to be felt did he instinctively relax the tight ball of his body and, opening out, touch her—not merely with his wetsuit-encased body, but with his unprotected hands and forehead.

The Youngest shuddered all through her length at that first contact. But before she could withdraw, his own reflexes operated. His chilling body felt warmth and did not stop to ask its source. Automatically, he huddled close against the surfaces he touched.

The Youngest bowed her head. It was too late. It was done.

This was no momentary, unconscious contact. She could feel his shivering directly now through her own skin surface. Nothing remained but to accept what had happened. She folded herself close about him, covering as much of his small, cold, trembling body as possible with her own warm surface, just as she would have if he had been a new hatchling who suffered from the chill. He gave a quavering sigh of relief and pressed close against her.

Gradually he warmed and his trembling stopped. Long before that, he had fallen into a deep, torpor-like slumber. She could hear the near-snores of his heavy breathing.

Grown bolder by contact with him and abandoning herself to an affection for him, she explored his slumbering shape with her sensitive cheek cells. He had no true swim paddles, of course—she already knew this about the upright animals. But she had never guessed how delicate and intricate were the several-times split appendages that he possessed on his upper limbs where swim paddles might have been. His body was very narrow, its skeleton hardly clothed in flesh. Now that she knew that his kind were as vulnerable to cold as new hatchlings, she did not wonder that it should be so with them: they had hardly anything over their bones to protect them from the temperature of the water and air. No wonder they covered themselves with non-living skins.

His head was not long at all, but quite round. His mouth was small and his jaws flat, so that he would be able to take only very small bites of things. There was a sort of protuberance above the mouth and a pair of eyes, side by side. Around the mouth and below the eyes his skin was full of tiny, sharp points; and on the top of his head was a strange, springy mat of very fine filaments. The Youngest rested the cells of her right cheek for a moment on the filaments, finding a strange inner warmth and pleasure in the touch of them. It was a completely inexplicable pleasure, for the legends had forgotten what old, primitive parts of her brain remembered: a time when her ancestors on land had worn fur and known the feel of it in their close body contacts.

Wrapped up in the subconscious evocation of ancient companionship, she lay in the darkness spinning impossible fantasies in which she would be able to keep him. He could live in this cave, she thought, and she would catch salmon—since that was what his kind, with their hooks and filaments, seemed most to search for—to bring to him for food. If he wanted "made" things about him, she could probably visit docks and suchlike about the loch and find some to bring here to him. When he got to know her better, since he had the things that let him hold his breath underwater, they could venture out into the loch together. Of course, once that time was reached, she would have to tell Second Mother and First Uncle about him. No doubt it would disturb them greatly, the fact that the taboo had been broken; but once they had met him underwater, and seen how sensible and friendly he was—how wise, even, for a small animal like himself . . .

Even as she lay dreaming these dreams, however, a sane part of her mind was still on duty. Realistically, she knew that what she was thinking was nonsense. Centuries of legend, duty, and taboo were not to be upset in a few days by any combination of accidents. Nor, even if no problem arose from the Family side, could she really expect him to live in a cave, forsaking his own species. His kind needed light as well as air. They needed the freedom to come and go on shore. Even if she could manage to keep him with her in the cave for a while, eventually the time would come when he would yearn for the land under his feet and the open sky overhead, at one and the same time. No, her imaginings could never be; and, because she knew this, when her internal time sense warned her that the night was nearly over, she silently uncoiled from around him and slipped back into the water, leaving the cave before the first light, which filtered in past the tree roots in the cave roof, could let him see who it was that had kept him alive through the hours of darkness.

Left uncovered on the ledge but warm again, he slept heavily on, unaware.

Out in the waters of the loch, in the pre-dawn gloom, the Youngest felt fatigue for the first time. She could easily go twenty-four hours without sleep; but this twenty-four hours just past had been emotionally charged ones. She had an irresistible urge to find one of the caves she favored herself and to lose herself in slumber. She shook it off. Before anything else, she must check with Second Mother.

Going swiftly to the new hatchhole, she found Second Mother fully awake, alert, and eager to talk to her. Evidently Second Mother had awakened early and spent some time thinking.

"You're young," she signaled the Youngest, "far too young to share the duty of guarding a clutch of eggs, even with someone as wise as your First Uncle. Happily, there's no problem physically. You're mature enough so that milk would come, if a hatchling should try to nurse from you. But, sensibly, you're still far too young to take on this sort of responsibility. Nonetheless, if something should happen to me, there would only be you and the Uncle to see this clutch to the hatching point. Therefore, we have to think of the possibility that you might have to take over for me."

"No. No, I couldn't," said the Youngest.

"You may have to. It's still only a remote possibility; but I should have taken it into consideration before. Since there're only the four of us, if anything happened to one of us, the remaining would have to see the eggs through to hatching. You and I could do it, I'm not worried about that situation. But with a clutch there must be a mother. Your uncle can be everything but that, and First Mother is really too old. Somehow, we must make you ready before your time to take on that duty."

"If you say so . . ." said the Youngest, unhappily.

"Our situation says so. Now, all you need to know, really, is told in the legends. But knowing them and understanding them are two different things . . ."

Then Second Mother launched into a retelling of the long chain of stories associated with the subject of eggs and hatchlings. The Youngest, of course, had heard them all before. More than that, she had them stored, signal by signal, in her memory as perfectly as had Second Mother herself. But she understood that Second Mother wanted her not only to recall each of these packages of stored wisdom, but to think about what was stated in them. Also—so much wiser had she already become in twenty-four hours—she realized that the events of yesterday had suddenly shocked Second Mother, giving her a feeling of helplessness should the upright animals ever really chance to stumble upon the hatchhole. For she could never abandon her eggs, and if she stayed with them the best she could hope for would be to give herself up to the land-dwellers in hope that this would satisfy them and they would look no further.

It was hard to try and ponder the legends, sleepy as the Youngest was, but she tried her best; and when at last Second Mother turned her loose, she swam groggily off to the nearest cave and curled up. It was now broad-enough daylight for her early feeding period, but she was too tired to think of food. In seconds, she was sleeping almost as deeply as the diver had been when she left him.

She came awake suddenly and was in motion almost before her eyes were open. First Uncle's signal of alarm was ringing all through the loch. She plunged from her cave into the outer waters. Vibrations told her that he and Second Mother were headed north, down the deep center of the loch as fast as they could travel, carrying the clutch of eggs. She drove on to join them, sending ahead her own signal that she was coming.

"Quick! Oh, quick!" signaled Second Mother.

Unencumbered, she began to converge on them at double their speed. Even in this moment her training paid off. She shot through the water, barely fifty feet above the bed of the loch, like a dolphin in the salt sea; and her perfect shape and smooth skin caused no turbulence at all to drag at her passage and slow her down.

She caught up with them halfway between Inverfarigaig and Dores and took her half of the eggs from Second Mother, leaving the older female free to find a new hatchhole. Unburdened, Second Mother leaped ahead and began to range the loch bed in search of a safe place.

"What happened?" signaled Youngest.

"Again!" First Uncle answered. "They dropped another 'made' thing, just like the first, almost in the hatchhole this time!" he told her.

Second Mother had been warming the eggs. Luckily he had been close. He had swept in; but not daring to break the line a second time for fear of giving clear evidence of the Family, he had simply scooped a hole in the loch bed, pushed the thing in, buried it and pressed down hard on the loch bed material with which he had covered it. He had buried it deeply enough so that the animals above were pulling up on their line with caution, for fear that they themselves might break it. Eventually, they would get it loose. Until then, the Family had a little time in which to find another location for the eggs.

A massive shape loomed suddenly out of the peaty darkness, facing them. It was First Mother, roused from her cave by the emergency.

"I can still carry eggs. Give them here, and you go back," she ordered First Uncle. "Find out what's being done with that 'made' thing you buried and what's going on with those creatures. Two hatchholes stumbled on in two days is too much for chance."

First Uncle swirled about and headed back.

The Youngest slowed down. First Mother was still tremendously powerful, of course, more so than any of them; but she no longer had the energy reserves to move at the speed at which First Uncle and the Youngest had been traveling. Youngest felt a surge of admiration for First Mother, battling the chill of the open loch water and the infirmities of her age to give help now, when the Family needed it.

"Here! This way!" Second Mother called.

They turned sharply toward the east bank of the loch and homed in on Second Mother's signal. She had found a good place for a new hatchhole. True, it was not near the mouth of a stream; but the loch bed was clean and this was one of the few spots where the rocky slope underwater from the shore angled backward when it reached a depth below four hundred feet, so that the loch at this point was actually in under the rock and had a roof overhead. Here, there was no way that a "made" thing could be dropped down on a line to come anywhere close to the hatchhole.

When First Mother and the Youngest got there, Second Mother was already at work making and cleaning the hole. The hole had barely been finished and Second Mother settled down with the clutch under her, when First Uncle arrived.

"They have their 'made' thing back," he reported. "They pulled on its line with little, repeated jerkings until they loosened it from its bed, and then they lifted it back up."

He told how he had followed it up through the water until he was just under the "made" thing and rode on the loch surface. Holding himself there, hidden by the thing itself, he had listened, trying to make sense out of what the animals were doing, from what he could hear.

They had made a great deal of noise after they hoisted the thing back on board. They had moved it around a good deal and done things with it, before finally leaving it alone and starting back toward the dock near St. Ninian's. First Uncle had followed them until he was sure that was where they were headed; then he had come to find the new hatchhole and the rest of the Family.

After he was done signaling, they all waited for First Mother to respond, since she was the oldest and wisest. She lay thinking for some moments.

"They didn't drop the 'made' thing down into the water again, you say?" she asked at last.

"No," signaled First Uncle.

"And none of them went down into the water, themselves?"

"No."

"It's very strange," said First Mother. "All we know is that they've twice almost found the hatchhole. All I can guess is that this isn't a chance thing, but that they're acting with some purpose. They may not be searching for our eggs, but they seem to be searching for *something*."

The Youngest felt a sudden chilling inside her. But First Mother was already signaling directly to First Uncle.

"From now on, you should watch them, whenever the thing in which they move about the loch surface isn't touching shore. If you need help, the Youngest can help you. If they show any signs of coming close to here, we must move the eggs immediately. I'll come out twice a day to relieve Second Mother for her feeding, so that you can be free to do that watching. No"—she signaled sharply before they could object—"I *will* do this. I can go for some days warming the eggs for two short periods a day, before I'll be out of strength; and this effort of mine is needed. The eggs *should* be safe here, but if it proves that the creatures have some means of finding them, wherever the hatchhole is placed in the open loch, we'll have to move the clutch into the caves."

Second Mother cried out in protest.

"I know," First Mother said, "the legends counsel against ever taking the eggs into the caves until time for hatching. But we may have no choice."

"My eggs will die!" wept Second Mother.

"They're your eggs, and the decision to take them inside has to be yours," said First Mother. "But they won't live if the animals find them. In the caves there may be a chance of life for them. Besides, our duty as a Family is to survive. It's the Family we have to think of, not a single clutch of eggs or a single individual. If worse comes to worst and it turns out we're not safe from the animals even in the caves, we'll try the journey of the Lost Father from Loch Morar before we'll let ourselves all be killed off."

"What Lost Father?" the Youngest demanded. "No one ever told me a legend about a Lost Father from Loch Morar. What's Loch Morar?"

"It's not a legend usually told to those too young to have full wisdom," said First Mother. "But these are new and dangerous times. Loch Morar is a loch a long way from here, and some of our People were also left there when the ice went and the land rose. They were of our People, but a different Family."

"But what about a Lost Father?" the Youngest persisted, because First Mother had stopped talking as if she would say no more about it. "How could a Father be lost?"

"He was lost to Loch Morar," First Mother explained, "because he grew old and died here in Loch Ness."

"But how did he get here?"

"He couldn't, that's the point," said First Uncle, grumpily. "There are legends *and* legends. That's why some are not told to young ones until they've matured enough to understand. The journey the Lost Father's supposed to have made is impossible. Tell it to some youngster and he or she's just as likely to try and duplicate it."

"But you said we might try it!" The Youngest appealed to First Mother.

"Only if there were no other alternative," First Mother answered. "I'd try flying out over the mountains if that was the only alternative left, because it's our duty to keep trying to survive as a Family as long as we're alive. So, as a last resort, we'd try the journey of the Lost Father, even though as the Uncle says, it's impossible."

"Why? Tell me what it was. You've already begun to tell me. Shouldn't I know all of it?"

"I suppose . . ." said First Mother, wearily. "Very well. Loch Morar isn't surrounded by mountains as we are here. It's even fairly close to the sea, so that if a good way could be found for such as us to travel over dry land, members of the People living there might be able to go home to the sea we all recall by the legends. Well, this legend says that there once was a Father in Loch Morar who dreamed all his life of leading his Family home to the sea. But we've grown too heavy nowadays to travel any distance overland, normally. One winter day, when a new snow had just fallen, the legend says this Father discovered a way of traveling on land that worked."

In sparse sentences, First Mother rehearsed the legend to a fascinated Youngest. It told that the snow provided a slippery surface over which the great bodies of the People could slide under the impetus of the same powerful tail muscles that drove them through the water, their swim paddles acting as rudders—or brakes—on downslopes. Actually, what the legend described was a way of swimming on land. Loch Ness never froze and First Mother therefore had no knowledge of ice-skating, so she could not explain that what the legend spoke of was the same principle that makes a steel ice blade glide over ice—the weight upon it causing the ice to melt under the sharp edge of the blade so that, effectively, it slides on a cushion of water. With the People, their ability to shunt a controlled amount of warmth to the skin in contact with the ice and snow did the same thing.

In the legend, the Father who discovered this tried to take his Family from Loch Morar back to the sea, but they were all afraid to try going, except for him. So he went alone and found his way to the ocean more easily than he had thought possible. He spent some years in the sea, but found it lonely and came back to land to return to Loch Morar. However, though it was winter, he could not find enough snow along the route he had taken to the sea in order to get back to Loch Morar. He hunted northward for a snow-covered route inland, north past the isle of Sleat, past Glenelg; and finally, under Benn Attow, he found a snow route that led him ultimately to Glen Moriston and into Loch Ness.

He went as far back south through Loch Ness as he could go, even trying some distance down what is now the southern part of the Caledonian Canal before he became convinced that the route back to Loch Morar by that way would be too long and hazardous to be practical. He decided to return to the sea and wait for snow to make him a way over his original route to Morar.

But, meanwhile, he had become needed in Loch Ness and grown fond of the Family there. He wished to take them with him to the sea. The others, however, were afraid to try the long overland journey; and while they hesitated and put off going, he grew too old to lead them; and so they never did go. Nevertheless, the legend told of his route and, memories being what they were among the People, no member of the Family in Loch Ness, after First Mother had finished telling the legend to the Youngest, could not have retraced the Lost Father's steps exactly.

"I don't think we should wait," the Youngest said, eagerly, when First Mother was through. "I think we should go now—I mean, as soon as we get a snow on the banks of the loch so that we can travel. Once we're away from the loch, there'll be snow all the time, because it's only the warmth of the loch that keeps the snow off around here. Then we could all go home to the sea, where be belong, away from the animals and their 'made' things. Most of the eggs laid there would hatch—"

"I told you so," First Uncle interrupted, speaking to First Mother. "Didn't I tell you so?"

"And what about my eggs now?" said Second Mother.

"We'll try something like that only if the animals start to destroy us," First Mother said to the Youngest with finality. "Not before. If it comes to that, Second Mother's present clutch of eggs will be lost, anyway. Otherwise, we'd never leave them, you should know that. Now, I'll go back to the cave and rest until late feeding period for Second Mother."

She went off. First Uncle also went off, to make sure that the animals had really gone to the dock and were still there. The Youngest, after asking Second Mother if there was any way she could be useful and being told there was none, went off to her delayed first feeding period.

She was indeed hungry, with the ravenous hunger of youth. But once she had taken the edge off her appetite, an uneasy feeling began to grow inside her, and not even stuffing herself with rich-fleshed salmon made it go away.

What was bothering her, she finally admitted to herself, was the sudden, cold thought that had intruded on her when First Mother had said that the creatures seemed to be searching for something. The Youngest was very much afraid she knew what they were searching for. It was their fellow, the diver she had taken to the cave. If she had not done anything, they would have found his body before this; but because she had saved him, they were still looking; and because he was in a cave, they could not find him. So they would keep on searching, and sooner or later they would come close to the new hatchhole; and then Second Mother would take the clutch into one of the caves, and the eggs would die, and it would be her own fault, the Youngest's fault alone.

She was crying inside. She did not dare cry out loud because the others would hear and want to know what was troubling her. She was ashamed to tell them what she had done. Somehow, she must put things right herself, without telling them—at least until some later time, when it would be all over and unimportant.

The diver must go back to his own people—if he had not already.

She turned and swam toward the cave, making sure to approach it from deep in the loch. Through the entrance of the cave, she stood up in the shallow interior pool and lifted her head out of water; and he was still there.

Enough light was filtering in through the ceiling cracks of the cave to make a sort of dim twilight inside. She saw him plainly—and he saw her.

She had forgotten that he would have no idea of what she looked like. He had been sitting up on the rock ledge; but when her head and its long neck rose out of the water, he stared and then scrambled back—as far back from her as he could get, to the rock wall of the cave behind the ledge. He stood pressed against it, still staring at her, his mouth open in a soundless circle.

She paused, irresolute. She had never intended to frighten him. She had forgotten that he might consider her at all frightening. All her foolish imaginings of keeping him here in the cave and of swimming with him in the loch crumbled before the bitter reality of his terror at the sight of her. Of course, he had had no idea of who had been coiled about him in the dark. He had only known that something large had been bringing the warmth of life back into him. But surely he would make the connection, now that he saw her?

She waited.

He did not seem to be making it. He simply stayed where he was, as if paralyzed by her presence. She felt an exasperation with him rising inside her. According to the legends, his kind had at least a share of intelligence, possibly even some aspect of wisdom, although that was doubtful. But now, crouched against the back of the cave, he looked like nothing more than another wild animal—like one of the otters, strayed from nearby streams, she had occasionally encountered in these caves. And as with such an otter, for all its small size ready to scratch or bite, she felt a caution about approaching him.

Nevertheless, something had to be done. At any moment now, the others like him would be out on the loch in their "made" thing, once more hunting for him and threatening to rediscover the hatchhole.

Cautiously, slowly, so as not to send him into a fighting reflex, she approached the ledge and crept up on it sideways, making an arc of her body and moving in until she half surrounded him, an arm's length from him. She was ready to pull back at the first sign of a hostile move, but no action was triggered in him. He merely stayed where he was, pressing against the rock wall as if he would like to step through it, his eyes fixed on her and his jaws still in the half-open position. Settled about him, however, she shunted blood into her skin area and began to radiate heat.

It took a little while for him to feel the warmth coming from her and some little while more to understand what she was trying to tell him. But then, gradually, his tense body relaxed. He slipped down the rock against which he was pressed and ended up sitting, gazing at her with a different shape to his eyes and mouth.

He made some noises with his mouth. These conveyed no sense to the Youngest, of course, but she thought that at least they did not sound like unfriendly noises.

"So now you know who I am," she signaled, although she knew perfectly well he could not understand her. "Now, you've got to swim out of here and go back on the land. Go back to your People."

She had corrected herself instinctively on the last term. She had been about to say "go back to the other animals"; but something inside her dictated the change—which was foolish, because he would not know the difference, anyway.

He straightened against the wall and stood up. Suddenly, he reached out an upper limb toward her.

She flinched from his touch instinctively, then braced herself to stay put. If she wanted him not to be afraid of her, she would have to show him the same fearlessness. Even the otters, if left alone, would calm down somewhat, though they would take the first opportunity to slip past and escape from the cave where they had been found.

She held still, accordingly. The divided ends of his limb touched her and rubbed lightly over her skin. It was not an unpleasant feeling, but she did not like it. It had been different when he was helpless and had touched her unconsciously.

She now swung her head down close to watch him and had the satisfaction of seeing him start when her own eyes and jaws came within a foot or so of his. He pulled his limbs back quickly, and made more noises. They were still not angry noises, though, and this fact, together with his quick withdrawal, gave her an impression that he was trying to be conciliatory, even friendly.

Well, at least she had his attention. She turned, backed off the ledge into the water, then reached up with her nose and pushed toward him the "made" things he originally had had attached to his back and head. Then, turning, she ducked under the water, swam out of the cave into the loch, and waited just under the surface for him to follow.

He did not.

She waited for more than enough time for him to reattach his things and make up his mind to follow, then she swam back inside. To her disgust, he was now sitting down again and his "made" things were still unattached to him.

She came sharply up to the edge of the rock and tumbled the two things literally on top of him.

"Put them on!" she signaled. "Put them on, you stupid animal!"

He stared at her and made noises with his mouth. He

stood up and moved his upper limbs about in the air. But he made no move to pick up the "made" things at his feet. Angrily, she shoved them against his lower limb ends once more.

He stopped making noises and merely looked at her. Slowly, although she could not define all of the changes that signaled it to her, an alteration of manner seemed to take place in him. The position of his upright body changed subtly. The noises he was making changed; they became slower and more separate, one from another. He bent down and picked up the larger of the things, the one that he had had attached to his back; but he did not put it on.

Instead, he held it up in the air before him as if drawing her attention to it. He turned it over in the air and shook it slightly, then held it in that position some more. He rapped it with the curled-over sections of one of his limb-ends, so that it rang with a hollow sound from both its doubled parts. Then he put it down on the ledge again and pushed it from him with one of his lower limb ends.

The Youngest stared at him, puzzled, but nonetheless hopeful for the first time. At last he seemed to be trying to communicate something to her, even though what he was doing right now seemed to make no sense. Could it be that this was some sort of game the upright animals played with their "made" things; and he either wanted to play it, or wanted her to play it with him, before he would put the things on and get in the water? When she was much younger, she had played with things herself— interesting pieces of rock or waterlogged material she found on the loch bed, or flotsam she had encountered on the surface at night, when it was safe to spend time in the open.

No, on second thought that explanation hardly seemed likely. If it was a game he wanted to play with her, it was more reasonable for him to push the things at her instead of just pushing the bigger one away and ignoring it. She watched him, baffled. Now he had picked up the larger thing again and was repeating his actions, exactly.

The creature went through the same motions several more times, eventually picking up and putting the smaller "made" thing about his head and muzzle, but still shaking and pushing away the larger thing. Eventually he made a louder noise which, for the first time, sounded really angry; threw the larger thing to one end of the ledge; and went off to sit down at the far end of the ledge, his back to her.

Still puzzled, the Youngest stretched her neck up over the ledge to feel the rejected "made" thing again with her cheek cells. It was still an enigmatic, cold, hard, double-shaped object that made no sense to her. What he's doing can't be playing, she thought. Not that he was playing at the last, there. And besides, he doesn't act as if he liked it and liked to play with it, he's acting as if he hated it—

Illumination came to her, abruptly.

"Of course!" she signaled at him.

But of course the signal did not even register on him. He still sat with his back to her.

What he had been trying to tell her, she suddenly realized, was that for some reason the "made" thing was no good for him any longer. Whether he had used it to play with, to comfort himself, or, as she had originally guessed, it had something to do with making it possible for him to stay underwater, for some reason it was now no good for that purpose.

The thought that it might indeed be something to help him stay underwater suddenly fitted in her mind with the fact that he no longer considered it any good. She sat back on her tail, mentally berating herself for being so foolish. Of course, that was what he had been trying to tell her. It would not help him stay underwater anymore; and to get out of the cave he had to go underwater—not very far, of course, but still a small distance.

On the other hand, how was he to know it was only a

small distance? He had been unconscious when she had brought him here.

Now that she had worked out what she thought he had been trying to tell her, she was up against a new puzzle. By what means was she to get across to him that she had understood?

She thought about this for a time, then picked up the thing in her teeth and threw it herself against the rock wall at the back of the ledge.

He turned around, evidently alerted by the sounds it made. She stretched out her neck, picked up the thing, brought it back to the water edge of the ledge, and then threw it at the wall again.

Then she looked at him.

He made sounds with his mouth and turned all the way around. Was it possible he had understood, she wondered? But he made no further moves, just sat there. She picked up and threw the "made" thing a couple of more times; then she paused once again to see what he might do.

He stood, hesitating, then inched forward to where the thing had fallen, picked up and threw it himself. But he threw it, as she had thrown it—at the rock wall behind the ledge.

The Youngest felt triumph. They were finally signaling each other—after a fashion.

But now where did they go from here? She wanted to ask him if there was anything they could do about the "made" thing being useless, but she could not think how to act that question out.

He, however, evidently had something in mind. He went to the edge of the rock shelf, knelt down and placed one of his multi-divided limb ends flat on the water surface, but with its inward-grasping surface upward. Then he moved it across the surface of the water so that the outer surface, or back, of it was in the water but the inner surface was still dry.

She stared at him. Once more he was doing something incomprehensible. He repeated the gesture several more times, but still it conveyed no meaning to her. He gave up, finally, and sat for a few minutes looking at her; then he got up, went back to the rock wall, turned around, walked once more to the edge of the ledge, and sat down.

Then he held up one of his upper limb ends with all but two of the divisions curled up. The two that were not curled up he pointed downward, and lowered them until their ends rested on the rock ledge. Then, pivoting first on the end of one of the divisions, then on the other, he moved the limb end back toward the wall as far as he could stretch, then turned it around and moved it forward again to the water's edge, where he folded up the two extended divisions, and held the limb end still.

He did this again. And again.

The Youngest concentrated. There was some meaning here; but with all the attention she could bring to bear on it, she still failed to see what it was. This was even harder than extracting wisdom from the legends. As she watched, he got up once more, walked back to the rock wall, came forward again and sat down. He did this twice.

Then he did the limb-end, two-division-movement thing twice.

Then he walked again, three times.

Then he did the limb-end thing three more times—

Understanding suddenly burst upon the Youngest. He was trying to make some comparison between his walking to the back of the ledge and forward again, and moving his limb ends in that odd fashion, first backward and then forward. The two divisions, with their little joints, moved much like his two lower limbs when he walked on them. It was extremely interesting to take part of your body and make it act like your whole body, doing something. Youngest wished that her swim paddles had divisions on the ends, like his, so she could try it.

She was becoming fascinated with the diver all over

again. She had almost forgotten the threat to the eggs that others like him posed as long as he stayed hidden in this cave. Her conscience caught her up sharply. She should check right now and see if things were all right with the Family. She turned to leave, and then checked herself. She wanted to reassure him that she was coming back.

For a second only she was baffled for a means to do this; then she remembered that she had already left the cave once, thinking he would follow her, and then come back when she had given up on his doing so. If he saw her go and come several times, he should expect that she would go on returning, even though the interval might vary.

She turned and dived out through the hole into the loch, paused for a minute or two, then went back in. She did this two more times before leaving the cave finally. He had given her no real sign that he understood what she was trying to convey, but he had already showed signs of that intelligence the legends credited his species with. Hopefully, he would figure it out. If he did not—well, since she was going back anyway, the only harm would be that he might worry a bit about being abandoned there.

She surfaced briefly, in the center of the loch, to see if many of the "made" things were abroad on it today. But none were in sight and there was little or no sign of activity on the banks. The sky was heavy with dark, low-lying clouds; and the hint of snow, heavy snow, was in the sharp air. She thought again of the journey of the Lost Father of Loch Morar, and of the sea it could take them to—their safe home, the sea. They should go. They should go without waiting. If only she could convince them to go . . .

She dropped by the hatchhole, found First Mother warming the eggs while Second Mother was off feeding, and heard from First Mother that the craft had not left its place on shore all day. Discussing this problem almost as equals with First Mother—of whom she had always been very much in awe—emboldened the Youngest to the point where she shyly suggested she might try warming the clutch herself, occasionally, so as to relieve First Mother from these twice-daily stints, which must end by draining her strength and killing her.

"It would be up to Second Mother, in any case," First Mother answered, "but you're still really too small to be sure of giving adequate warmth to a full clutch. In an emergency, of course, you shouldn't hesitate to do your best with the eggs, but I don't think we're quite that desperate, yet."

Having signaled this, however, First Mother apparently softened.

"Besides," she said, "the time to be young and free of responsibilities is short enough. Enjoy it while you can. With the Family reduced to the four of us and this clutch, you'll have a hard enough adulthood, even if Second Mother manages to produce as many as two hatchlings out of the five or six clutches she can still have before her laying days are over. The odds of hatching females over males are four to one; but still, it could be that she might produce only a couple of males—and then everything would be up to you. So, use your time in your own way while it's still yours to use. But keep alert. If you're called, come immediately!"

The Youngest promised that she would. She left First Mother and went to find First Uncle, who was keeping watch in the neighborhood of the dock to which the craft was moored. When she found him, he was hanging in the loch about thirty feet deep and about a hundred feet offshore from the craft, using his sensitive hearing to keep track of what was happening in the craft and on the dock.

"I'm glad you're here," he signaled to the Youngest when she arrived. "It's time for my second feeding; and I think there're none of the animals on the 'made' thing, right now. But it wouldn't hurt to keep a watch, anyway. Do you want to stay here and listen while I go and feed?"

Actually, Youngest was not too anxious to do so. Her plan had been to check with the Uncle, then do some feeding herself and get back to her diver while daylight was still coming into his cave. But she could hardly explain that to First Uncle.

"Of course," she said. "I'll stay here until you get back."

"Good," said the Uncle; and went off.

Left with nothing to do but listen and think, the Youngest hung in the water. Her imagination, which really required very little to start it working, had recaptured the notion of making friends with the diver. It was not so important, really, that he had gotten a look at her. Over the centuries a number of incidents had occurred in which members of the Family were seen briefly by one or more of the animals, and no bad results had come from those sightings. But it was important that the land-dwellers not realize there was a true Family. If she could just convince the diver that she was the last and only one of her People, it might be quite safe to see him from time to time—of course, only when he was alone and when they were in a safe place of her choosing, since though he might be trustworthy, his fellows who had twice threatened the hatchhole clearly were not.

The new excitement about getting to know him had come from starting to be able to "talk" with him. If she and he kept at it, they could probably work out ways to tell all sorts of things to each other eventually.

That thought reminded her that she had not yet figured out why it was important to him that she understand that moving his divided limb ends in a certain way could stand for his walking. He must have had some reason for showing her that. Maybe it was connected with his earlier moving of his limb ends over the surface of the water?

Before she had a chance to ponder the possible connection, a sound from above, reaching down through the water, alerted her to the fact that some of the creatures were once more coming out onto the dock. She drifted in closer, and heard the sounds move to the end of the dock and onto the craft.

Apparently, they were bringing something heavy aboard, because along with the noise of their lower limb ends on the structure came the thumping and rumbling of something which ended at last—to judge from the sounds—somewhere up on the forward deck where she had examined the box with the sloping top and the other "made" thing in the bow.

Following this, she heard some more sounds moving from the foredeck area into the cabin.

A little recklessly, the Youngest drifted in until she was almost under the craft and only about fifteen feet below the surface, and so verified that it was, indeed, in that part of the boat where the box with the sloping box stood that most of the activity was going on. Then the noise in that area slowed down and stopped, and she heard the sound of the animals walking back off the craft, down the dock and ashore. Things became once more silent.

First Uncle had not yet returned. The Youngest wrestled with her conscience. She had not been specifically told not to risk coming up to the surface near the dock; but she knew that was simply because it had not occurred to any of the older members of the Family that she would be daring enough to do such a thing. Of course, she had never told any of them how she had examined the foredeck of the craft once before. But now, having already done so, she had a hard time convincing herself it was too risky to do again. After all, hadn't she heard the animals leave the area? No matter how quiet one of them might try to be, her hearing was good enough to pick up little sounds of his presence, if he was still aboard.

In the end, she gave in to temptation—which is not to say she moved without taking every precaution. She drifted in, underwater, so slowly and quietly that a little crowd of curious minnows formed around her. Approaching the foredeck from the loch side of the craft, she stayed well underwater until she was right up against the hull. Touching it, she hung in the water, listening. When she still heard nothing, she lifted her head quickly, just enough for a glimpse over the side; then she ducked back under again and shot away and down to a safe distance.

Eighty feet deep and a hundred feet offshore, she paused to consider what she had seen.

Her memory, like that of everyone in the Family, was essentially photographic when she concentrated on remembering, as she had during her brief look over the side of the craft. But being able to recall exactly what she had looked at was not the same thing as realizing its import. In this case, what she had been looking for was what had just been brought aboard. By comparing what she had just seen with what she had observed on her night visit earlier, she had hoped to pick out any addition to the "made" things she had noted then.

At first glance, no difference had seemed visible. She noticed the box with the sloping top and the thing in the bow with the barbed rod inside. A number of other, smaller things were about the deck, too, some of which she had examined briefly the time before and some that she had barely noticed. Familiar were several of the doubled things like the one the diver had thrown from him in order to open up communications between them at first. Largely unfamiliar were a number of smaller boxes, some round things, other things that were combinations of round and angular shapes, and a sort of tall open frame, upright and holding several rods with barbed ends like the ones which the thing in the bow contained.

She puzzled over the assortment of things—and then without warning an answer came. But provokingly, as often happened with her, it was not the answer to the question she now had, but to an earlier one.

It had suddenly struck her that the diver's actions in rejecting the "made" thing he had worn on his back, and all his original signals to her, might mean that for some reason it was not the one he wanted, or needed, in order to leave the cave. Why there should be that kind of difference between it and these things left her baffled. The one with him now in the cave had been the right one; but maybe it was not the right one, today. Perhaps—she had a sudden inspiration—"made" things could die like animals or fish, or even like People, and the one he now had was dead. In any case, maybe what he needed was another of that particular kind of thing.

Perhaps this insight had come from the fact that several of these same "made" things were on the deck; and also, there was obviously only one diver, since First Uncle had not reported any of the other animals going down into the water. She was immediately tempted to go and get another one of the things, so that she could take it back to the diver. If he put it on, that meant she was right. Even if he did not, she might learn something by the way he handled it.

If it had been daring to take one look at the deck, it was inconceivably so to return now and actually try to take something from it. Her sense of duty struggled with her inclinations but slowly was overwhelmed. After all, she knew now—knew positively—that none of the animals were aboard the boat and none could have come aboard in the last few minutes because she was still close enough to hear them. But if she went, she would have to hurry if she was going to do it before the Uncle got back and forbade any such action.

She swam back to the craft in a rush, came to the surface beside it, rose in the water, craned her neck far enough inboard to snatch up one of the things in her teeth and escape with it.

A few seconds later, she had it two hundred feet down on the bed of the loch and was burying it in silt. Three minutes later she was back on station watching the craft, calmly enough but with her heart beating fast.

Happily, there was still no sign of First Uncle's return.

Her heartbeat slowed. She went back to puzzling over what it was on the foredeck that could be the thing she had heard the creatures bring aboard. Of course, she now had three memory images of the area to compare . . .

Recognition came.

There *was* a discrepancy between the last two mental images and the first one, a discrepancy about one of the "made" things to which she had devoted close attention, that first time.

The difference was the line attached to the box with the sloping top. It was not the same line at all. It was a drum of other line at least twice as thick as the one which had connected the heavy thing and the box previously—almost as thick as the thick line connecting the barbed rod to the thing in the bow that contained it. Clearly, the animals of the craft had tried to make sure that they would run no danger of losing their dropweight if it became buried again. Possibly they had foolishly hoped that it was so strong that not even First Uncle could break it as he had the first.

That meant they were not going to give up. Here was clear evidence they were going to go on searching for their diver. She *must* get him back to them as soon as possible.

She began to swim restlessly, to and fro in the underwater, anxious to see the Uncle return so that she could tell him what had been done.

He came not long afterward, although it seemed to her that she had waited and worried for a considerable time before he appeared. When she told him about the new line, he was concerned enough by the information so that he barely reprimanded her for taking the risk of going in close to the craft.

"I must tell First Mother, right away—" He checked himself and looked up through the twenty or so feet of water that covered them. "No, there're only a few more hours of daylight left. I need to think, anyway. I'll stay on guard here until dark, then I'll go see First Mother in her cave. Youngest, for right now don't say anything to Second Mother, or even to First Mother if you happen to talk to her. I'll tell both of them myself after I've had time to think about it."

"Then I can go now?" asked the Youngest, almost standing on her tail in the underwater in her eagerness to be off.

"Yes, yes," signaled the Uncle.

The Youngest turned and dove toward the spot where she had buried the "made" thing she had taken and about which she had been careful to say nothing to First Uncle. She had no time to explain about the diver now, and any mention of the thing would bring demands for a full explanation from her elders. Five minutes later, the thing in her teeth, she was splitting the water in the direction of the cave where she had left the diver.

She had never meant to leave him alone this long. An irrational fear grew in her that something had happened to him in the time she had been gone. Perhaps he had started chilling again and had lost too much warmth, like one of the old ones, and was now dead. If he was dead, would the other animals be satisfied just to have his body back? But she did not want to think of him dead: He was not a bad little animal, in spite of his acting in such an ugly fashion when he had seen her for the first time. She should have realized that in the daylight, seeing her as he had without warning for the first time—

The thought of daylight reminded her that First Uncle had talked about there being only a few hours of it left. Surely there must be more than that. The day could not have gone so quickly.

She took a quick slant up to the surface to check. No, she was right. There must be at least four hours yet before the sun would sink below the mountains. However, in his own way the Uncle had been right, also, because the clouds were very heavy now. It would be too dark to see much, even long before actual nightfall. Snow was certain by dark, possibly even before. As she floated for a moment with her head and neck out of water, a few of the first wandering flakes came down the wind and touched her right cheek cells with tiny, cold fingers.

She dived again. It would indeed be a heavy snowfall; the Family could start out tonight on their way to the sea, if only they wanted to. It might even be possible to carry the eggs, distributed among the four of them, just two or three carried pressed between a swim paddle and warm body skin. First Mother might tire easily; but after the first night, when they had gotten well away from the loch, and with new snow falling to cover their footsteps, they could go by short stages. There would be no danger that the others would run out of heat or strength. Even the Youngest, small as she was, had fat reserves for a couple of months without eating and with ordinary activity. The Lost Father had made it to Loch Ness from the sea in a week or so.

If only they would go now. If only she were old enough and wise enough to convince them to go. For just a moment she gave herself over to a dream of their great sea home, of the People grown strong again, patrolling in their great squadrons past the white-gleaming berg ice or under the tropic stars. Most of the eggs of every clutch would hatch, then. The hatchlings would have the beaches of all the empty islands of the world to hatch on. Later, in the sea, they would grow up strong and safe, with their mighty elders around to guard them from anything that moved in the salt waters. In their last years, the old ones would bask under the hot sun in warm, hidden places and never need to chill again. The sea. That was where they belonged. Where they must go home to, someday. And that day should be soon . . .

The Youngest was almost to the cave now. She brought her thoughts, with a wrench, back to the diver. Alive or dead, he too must go back—to his own kind. Fervently, she hoped that she was right about another "made" thing being what he needed before he would swim out of the cave. If not, if he just threw this one away as he had the other one, then she had no choice. She would simply have to pick him up in her teeth and carry him out of the cave without it. Of course, she must be careful to hold him so that he could not reach her to scratch or bite; and she must get his head back above water as soon as they got out of the cave into the open loch, so that he would not drown.

By the time she had gotten this far in her thinking, she was at the cave. Ducking inside, she exploded up through the surface of the water within. The diver was seated with his back against the cave wall, looking haggard and savage. He was getting quite dark-colored around the jaws, now. The little points he had there seemed to be growing. She dumped the new "made" thing at his feet.

For a moment he merely stared down at it, stupidly. Then he fumbled the object up into his arms and did something to it with those active little divided sections of his two upper limb ends. A hissing sound came from the thing that made her start back, warily. So, the "made" things were alive, after all!

The diver was busy attaching to himself the various things he had worn when she had first found him—with the exception that the new thing she had brought him, rather than its old counterpart, was going on his back. Abruptly, though, he stopped, his head-thing still not on and still in the process of putting on the paddle-like things that attached to his lower limb ends. He got up and came forward to the edge of the water, looking at her.

He had changed again. From the moment he had gotten the new thing to make the hissing noise, he had gone into yet a different way of standing and acting. Now he came within limb reach of her and stared at her so self-assuredly that she almost felt she was the animal trapped in a cave and he was free. Then he crouched down by the water and once more began to make motions with his upper limbs and limb ends.

First, he made the on-top-of-the-water sliding motion with the back of one limb end that she now began to understand must mean the craft he had gone overboard from. Once she made the connection it was obvious: the craft, like his hand, was in the water only with its underside. Its top side was dry and in the air. As she watched, he circled his "craft" limb end around in the water and brought it back to touch the ledge. Then, with his other limb end, he "walked" two of its divisions up to the "craft" and continued to "walk" them onto it.

She stared. He was apparently signaling something about his getting on the craft. But why?

However, now he was doing something else. He lifted his walking-self limb end off the "craft" and put it standing on its two stiff divisions, back on the ledge. Then he moved the "craft" out over the water, away from the ledge, and held it there. Next, to her surprise, he "walked" his other limb end right off the ledge into the water. Still "walking" so that he churned the still surface of the cave water to a slight roughness, he moved that limb end slowly to the unmoving "craft." When the "walking" limb end reached the "craft," it once more stepped up onto it.

The diver now pulled his upper limbs back, sat crouched on the ledge, and looked at the Youngest for a long moment. Then he made the same signals again. He did it a third time, and she began to understand. He was showing himself swimming to his craft. Of course, he had no idea how far he actually was from it, here in the cave—an unreasonable distance for as weak a swimmer as one of his kind was.

But now he was signaling yet something else. His "walking" limb end stood at the water's edge. His other limb end was not merely on the water, but in it, below the surface. As she watched, a single one of that other limb end's divisions rose through the surface and stood, slightly crooked, so that its upper joint was almost at right angles to the part sticking through the surface. Seeing her gaze on this part of him, the diver began to move that solitary joint through the water in the direction its crooked top was pointing. He brought it in this fashion all the way to the rock ledge and halted it opposite the "walking" limb end standing there.

He held both limb ends still in position and looked at her, as if waiting for a sign of understanding.

She gazed back, once more at a loss. The joint sticking up out of the water was like nothing in her memory but the limb of a waterlogged tree, its top more or less looking at the "walking" limb end that stood for the diver. But if the "walking" limb end was *he*—? Suddenly she understood. The division protruding from the water signalized *her!*

To show she understood, she backed off from the ledge, crouched down in the shallow water of the cave until nothing but her upper neck and head protruded from the water, and then—trying to look as much like his crooked division as possible—approached him on the ledge.

He made noises. There was no way of being sure, of course, but she felt she was beginning to read the tone of some of the sounds he made; and these latest sounds, she was convinced, sounded pleased and satisfied.

He tried something else.

He made the "walking" shape on the ledge, then added something. In addition to the two limb-end divisions standing on the rock, he unfolded another—a short, thick division, one at the edge of that particular limb end, and moved it in circular fashion, horizontally. Then he stood up on the ledge himself and swung one of his upper limbs at full length, in similar, circular fashion. He did this several times.

In no way could she imitate that kind of gesture, though she comprehended immediately that the movement of the extra, short division above the "walking" form was supposed to indicate him standing and swinging his upper limb like now. She merely stayed as she was and waited to see what he would do next.

He got down by the water, made the "craft" shape,

"swam" his "walking" shape to it, climbed the "walking" shape up on the "craft," then had the "walking" shape turn and make the upper-limb swinging motion.

The Youngest watched, puzzled, but caught up in this strange game of communication she and the diver had found to play together. Evidently he wanted to go back to his craft, get on it, and then wave his upper limb like that, for some reason. It made no sense so far—but he was already doing something more.

He now had the "walking" shape standing on the ledge, making the upper-limb swinging motion, and he was showing the crooked division that was she approaching through the water.

That was easy: he wanted her to come to the ledge when he swung his upper limb.

Sure enough, after a couple of demonstrations of the last shape signals, he stood up on the ledge and swung his arm. Agreeably, she went out in the water, crouched down, and approached the ledge. He made pleased noises. This was all rather ridiculous, she thought, but enjoyable nonetheless. She was standing half her length out from the edge, where she had stopped, and was trying to think of a body signal she could give that would make him swim to her, when she noticed that he was going on to further signals.

He had his "walking" shape standing on the "craft" shape, in the water out from the ledge, and signaling "Come." But then he took his "walking" shape away from the "craft" shape, put it under the water a little distance off, and came up with it as the "her" shape. He showed the "her" shape approaching the "craft" shape with her neck and head out of water.

She was to come to his craft? In response to his "Come" signal?

No!

She was so furious with him for suggesting such a thing that she had no trouble at all thinking of a way to convey her reaction. Turning around, she plunged underwater, down through the cave entrance and out into the loch. Her first impulse was to flash off and leave him there to do whatever he wanted—stay forever, go back to his kind, or engage in any other nonsensical activity his small head could dream up. Did he think she had no wisdom at all? To suggest that she come right up to his craft with her head and neck out of water when he signaled—as if there had never been a taboo against her People having anything to do with his! He must not understand her in the slightest degree.

Common sense caught up with her, halted her, and turned her about not far from the cave mouth. Going off like this would do her no good—more, it would do the Family no good. On the other hand, she could not bring herself to go back into the cave, now. She hung in the water, undecided, unable to conquer the conscience that would not let her swim off, but also unable to make herself re-enter.

Vibrations from the water in the cave solved her problem. He had evidently put on the "made" thing she had brought him and was coming out. She stayed where she was, reading the vibrations.

He came to the mouth of the cave and swam slowly, straight up, to the surface. Level with him, but far enough away to be out of sight in the murky water, the Youngest rose, too. He lifted his head at last into the open air and looked around him.

He's looking for me, thought the Youngest, with a sense of satisfaction that he would see no sign of her and would assume she had left him for good. Now, go ashore and go back to your own kind, she commanded in her thoughts.

But he did not go ashore, though shore was only a matter of feet from him. Instead, he pulled his head underwater once more and began to swim back down.

She almost exploded with exasperation. He was headed toward the cave mouth! He was going back inside!

"You stupid animal!" she signaled to him. *"Go ashore!"*

But of course he did not even perceive the signal, let alone understand it. Losing all patience, the Youngest swooped down upon him, hauled him to the surface once more, and let him go.

For a second he merely floated there, motionless, and she felt a sudden fear that she had brought him up through the water too swiftly. She knew of some small fish that spent all their time down in the deepest parts of the loch, and if you brought one of them too quickly up the nine hundred feet or so to the surface, it twitched and died, even though it had been carried gently. Sometimes part of the insides of these fish bulged out through their mouths and gill slits after they were brought up quickly.

After a second, the diver moved and looked at her.

Concerned for him, she had stayed on the surface with him, her head just barely out of the water. Now he saw her. He kicked with the "made" paddles on his lower limbs to raise himself partly out of the water and, a little awkwardly, with his upper limb ends made the signal of him swimming to his craft.

She did not respond. He did it several more times, but she stayed stubbornly non-communicative. It was bad enough that she had let him see her again after his unthinkable suggestion.

He gave up making signals. Ignoring the shore close at hand, he turned from her and began to swim slowly south and out into the center of the loch.

He was going in the wrong direction if he was thinking of swimming all the way to his craft. And after his signaling it was pretty clear that this was what he had in mind. Let him find out his mistake for himself, the Youngest thought, coldly.

But she found that she could not go through with that. Angrily, she shot after him, caught the thing on his back with her teeth, and, lifting him by it enough so that his head was just above the surface, began to swim with him in the right direction.

She went slowly—according to her own ideas of

speed—but even so a noticeable bow wave built up before him. She lifted him a little higher out of the water to be on the safe side; but she did not go any faster: perhaps he could not endure too much speed. As it was, the clumsy shape of his small body hung about with "made" things was creating surprising turbulence for its size. It was a good thing the present hatchhole (and, therefore, First Mother's current resting cave and the area in which First Uncle and Second Mother would do their feeding) was as distant as they were; otherwise First Uncle, at least, would certainly have been alarmed by the vibrations and have come to investigate.

It was also a good thing that the day was as dark as it was, with its late hour and the snow that was now beginning to fall with some seriousness; otherwise she would not have wanted to travel this distance on the surface in daylight. But the snow was now so general that both shores were lost to sight in its white, whirling multitudes of flakes, and certainly no animal on shore would be able to see her and the diver out here.

There was privacy and freedom, being hidden by the snow like this—like the freedom she felt on dark nights when the whole loch was free of the animals and all hers. If only it could be this way all the time. To live free and happy was so good. Under conditions like these, she could not even fear or dislike the animals, other than her diver, who were a threat to the Family.

At the same time, she remained firm in her belief that the Family should go, now. None of the others had ever before told her that any of the legends were untrustworthy, and she did not believe that the one about the Lost Father was so. It was not that that legend was untrustworthy, but that they had grown conservative with age and feared to leave the loch; while she, who was still young, still dared to try great things for possibly great rewards.

She had never admitted it to the older ones, but one midwinter day when she had been very young and quite small—barely old enough to be allowed to swim around in the loch by herself—she had ventured up one of the streams flowing into the loch. It was a stream far too shallow for an adult of the Family; and some distance up it, she found several otters playing on an ice slide they had made. She had joined them, sliding along with them for half a day without ever being seen by any upright animal. She remembered this all very well, particularly her scrambling around on the snow to get to the head of the slide; and that she had used her tail muscles to skid herself along on her warm belly surface, just as the Lost Father had described.

If she could get the others to slip ashore long enough to try the snowy loch banks before day-warmth combined with loch-warmth to clear them of the white stuff . . . But even as she thought this, she knew they would never agree to try. They would not even consider the journey home to the sea until, as First Mother said, it became clear that that was the only alternative to extinction at the hands of the upright animals.

It was a fact, and she must face it. But maybe she could think of some way to make plain to them that the animals had, indeed, become that dangerous. For the first time, it occurred to her that her association with the diver could turn out to be something that would help them all. Perhaps, through him, she could gain evidence about his kind that would convince the rest of the Family that they should leave the loch.

It was an exciting thought. It would do no disservice to him to use him in that fashion, because clearly he was different from others of his kind: he had realized that not only was she warm as he was, but as intelligent or more so than he. He would have no interest in being a danger to her People, and might even cooperate—if she could make him understand what she wanted—in convincing the Family of the dangers his own race posed to them. Testimony from one of the animals directly would be an argument to convince even First Uncle.

For no particular reason, she suddenly remembered

how he had instinctively huddled against her when he had discovered her warming him. The memory roused a feeling of tenderness in her. She found herself wishing there were some way she could signal that feeling to him. But they were almost to his craft, now. It and the dock were beginning to be visible—dark shapes lost in the dancing white—with the dimmer dark shapes of trees and other things ashore behind them.

Now that they were close enough to see a shore, the falling snow did not seem so thick, nor so all-enclosing as it had out in the middle of the loch. But there was still a privacy to the world it created, a feeling of security. Even sounds seemed to be hushed.

Through the water, Youngest could feel vibrations from the craft. At least one, possibly two, of the other animals were aboard it. As soon as she was close enough to be sure her diver could see the craft, she let go of the thing on his back and sank abruptly to about twenty feet below the surface, where she hung and waited, checking the vibrations of his movements to make sure he made it safely to his destination.

At first, when she let him go, he trod water where he was and turned around and around as if searching for her. He pushed himself up in the water and made the "Come" signal several times; but she refused to respond. Finally, he turned and swam to the edge of the craft.

He climbed on board very slowly, making so little noise that the two in the cabin evidently did not hear him. Surprisingly, he did not seem in any hurry to join them or to let them know he was back.

The Youngest rose to just under the surface and lifted her head above to see what he was doing. He was still standing on the foredeck, where he had climbed aboard, not moving. Now, as she watched, he walked heavily forward to the bow and stood beside the "made" thing there, gazing out in her direction.

He lifted his arm as if to make the "Come" signal, then dropped it to his side.

The Youngest knew that in absolutely no way could he make out the small portion of her head above the waves, with the snow coming down the way it was and day drawing swiftly to its dark close. She stared at him. She noticed something weary and sad about the way he stood. I should leave now, she thought. But she did not move. With the other two animals still unaware in the cabin, and the snow continuing to fall, there seemed no reason to hurry off. She would miss him, she told herself, feeling a sudden pang of loss. Looking at him, it came to her suddenly that from the way he was acting he might well miss her, too.

Watching, she remembered how he had half lifted his limb as if to signal and then dropped it again. Maybe his limb is tired, she thought.

A sudden impulse took her. I'll go in close, underwater, and lift my head high for just a moment, she thought, so he can see me. He'll know then that I haven't left him for good. He already understands I wouldn't come on board that thing of his under any circumstance. Maybe if he sees me again for a second, now, he'll understand that if he gets back in the water and swims to me, we can go on learning signals from each other. Then, maybe, someday, we'll know enough signals together so that he can convince the older ones to leave.

Even as she thought this, she was drifting in, underwater, until she was only twenty feet from the craft. She rose suddenly and lifted her head and neck clear of the water.

For a long second, she saw he was staring right at her but not responding. Then she realized that he might not be seeing her, after all, just staring blindly out at the loch and the snow. She moved a little sideways to attract his attention, and saw his head move. Then he *was* seeing her? Then why didn't he do something?

She wondered if something was wrong with him. After all, he had been gone for nearly two days from his own People and must have missed at least a couple of his feeding periods in that time. Concern impelled her to a closer look at him. She began to drift in toward the boat.

He jerked upright suddenly and swung an upper limb at her.

But he was swinging it all wrong. It was not the "Come" signal he was making, at all. It was more like the "Come" signal in reverse—as if he was pushing her back and away from him. Puzzled, and even a little hurt, because the way he was acting reminded her of how he had acted when he first saw her in the cave and did not know she had been with him earlier, the Youngest moved in even closer.

He flung both his upper limbs furiously at her in that new, "rejecting" motion and shouted at her—a loud, angry noise. Behind him, came an explosion of different noise from inside the cabin, and the other two animals burst out onto the deck. Her diver turned, making noises, waving both his limbs at them the way he had just waved them at her. The Youngest, who had been about to duck down below the safety of the loch surface, stopped. Maybe this was some new signal he wanted her to learn, one that had some reference to his two companions?

But the others were making noises back at him. The taller one ran to one of the "made" things that were like, but smaller than, the one in the bow of the boat. The diver shouted again, but the tall one ignored him, only seizing one end of the thing he had run to and pulling that end around toward him. The Youngest watched, fascinated, as the other end of the "made" thing swung to point at her.

Then the diver made a very large angry noise, turned, and seized the end of the largest "made" thing before him in the bow of the boat.

Frightened suddenly, for it had finally sunk in that for some reason he had been signaling her to get away, she turned and dived. Then, as she did so, she realized that she had turned, not away from, but into line with, the outer end of the thing in the bow of the craft.

She caught a flicker of movement, almost too fast to see, from the thing's hollow outer end. Immediately, the loudest sound she had ever heard exploded around her, and a tremendous blow struck her behind her left shoulder as she entered the underwater.

She signaled for help instinctively, in shock and fear, plunging for the deep bottom of the loch. From far off, a moment later, came the answer of First Uncle. Blindly, she turned to flee to him.

As she did, she thought to look and see what had happened to her. Swinging her head around, she saw a long, but shallow, gash across her shoulder and down her side. Relief surged in her. It was not even painful yet, though it might be later; but it was nothing to cripple her, or even to slow her down.

How could her diver have done such a thing to her? The thought was checked almost as soon as it was born—by the basic honesty of her training. *He* had not done this. *She* had done it, by diving into the path of the barbed rod cast from the thing in the bow. If she had not done that, it would have missed her entirely.

But why should he make the thing throw the barbed rod at all? She had thought he had come to like her, as she liked him.

Abruptly, comprehension came; and it felt as if her heart leaped in her. For all at once it was perfectly clear what he had been trying to do. She should have had more faith in him. She halted her flight toward the Uncle and turned back toward the boat.

Just below it, she found what she wanted. The barbed rod, still leaving a taste of her blood in the water, was hanging point down from its line, in about two hundred feet of water. It was being drawn back up, slowly but steadily.

She surged in close to it, and her jaws clamped on the line she had tried to bite before and found resistant. But now she was serious in her intent to sever it. Her jaws scissored and her teeth ripped at it, though she was careful to rise with the line and put no strain upon it that would warn the animals above about what she was doing. The tough strands began to part under her assault.

Just above her, the sound of animal noises now came clearly through the water: her diver and the others making sounds at each other.

" . . . I tell you we're through!" It was her diver speaking. "It's over. I don't care what you saw. It's my boat. I paid for it; and I'm quitting."

"It not *your* boat, man. It a boat belong to the company, the company that belong all three of us. We got contracts."

"I'll pay off your damned contracts."

"There's more to this than money, now. We know that great beast in there, now. We get our contract money, and maybe a lot more, going on the TV telling how we catch it and bring it in. No, man, you don't stop us now."

"I say, it's my boat. I'll get a lawyer and court order—"

"You do that. You get a lawyer and a judge and a pretty court order, and we'll give you the boat. You do that. Until then, it belong to the company and it keep after that beast."

She heard the sound of footsteps—her diver's footsteps, she could tell, after all this time of seeing him walk his lower limbs—leaving the boat deck, stepping onto the dock, going away.

The line was almost parted. She and the barbed rod were only about forty feet below the boat.

"What'd you have to do that for?" That was the voice of the third creature. "He'll do that! He'll get a lawyer and take the boat and we won't even get our minimum pay. Whyn't you let him pay us off, the way he said?"

"Hush, you fooking fool. How long you think it take him get a lawyer, a judge, and a writ? Four days, maybe five—"

The line parted. She caught the barbed rod in her

jaws as it started to sink. The ragged end of the line lifted and vanished above her.

"—and meanwhile, you and me, we go hunting with this boat. We know the beast there, now. We know what to look for. We find it in four, five day, easy."

"But even if we get it, he'll just take it away from us again with his lawyer—"

"I tell you, no. We'll get ourselves a lawyer, also. This company formed to take the beast; and he got to admit he tried to call off the hunt. And we both seen what he do. He've fired that harpoon gun to scare it off, so I can't get it with the drug lance and capture it. We testify to that, we got him—Ah!"

"What is it?"

"What is it? You got no eyes, man? The harpoon gone. It in that beast after all, being carried around. We don't need no four, five days, I tell you now. That be a good, long piece of steel, and we got the locators to find metal like that. We hunt that beast and bring it in tomorrow. Tomorrow, man, I promise you! It not going to go too fast, too far, with that harpoon."

But he could not see below the snow and the black surface of the water. The Youngest was already moving very fast indeed through the deep loch to meet the approaching First Uncle. In her jaws she carried the harpoon, and on her back she bore the wound it had made. The elders could have no doubt, now, about the intentions of the upright animals (other than her diver) and their ability to destroy the Family.

They must call First Mother, and this time there would be no hesitation. She would see the harpoon and the wound and decide for them all. Tonight they would leave by the route of the Lost Father, while the snow was still thick on the banks of the loch. They might have to leave the eggs behind, after all; but if so, Second Mother could have more clutches, and maybe later they would even find a way ashore again to Loch Morar and meet others of their own People at last.

But, in any case, they would go now to live free in

the sea; and in the sea most of Second Mother's future eggs would hatch and the Family would grow numerous and strong again.

She could see them in her mind's eye, now. They would leave the loch by the mouth of Glen Moriston—First Mother, Second Mother, First Uncle, herself—and take to the snow-covered banks when the water became too shallow . . .

They would travel steadily into the mountains, and the new snow falling behind them would hide the marks of their going from the eyes of the animals. They would pass by deserted ways through the silent rocks to the ocean. They would come at last to its endless waters, to the shining bergs of the north and the endless warmth of the Equator sun. The ocean, their home, was welcoming them back, at last. There would be no more doubt, no more fear or waiting. They were going home to the sea . . . they were going home to the sea . . . ☆

The Greenhouse Defect

Andrew J. Offutt

1

A dull blue in the sunlight, the old VW panted out of
the cool, dim lane flanked by lines of trees. Almost directly ahead sprawled the brick-and-redwood-and-glass
house, large and yet still an anomaly—though a lovely
one—in this area of colonnaded colonials and huge
barns as handsome and well-kept as the homes. The
house at the end of the gravel road was an island amid
thick grass and shrubs, trees and flowerbeds. All but
the last were vehemently green, even this early in May.
The trees were beyond the budding stage, the delicately
beautiful redbuds within a couple of days of losing their
Easter outfits of rosy pink.

A little wind, Judith mused, *anything above a breeze,
or a shower—and that's it for the Judas trees for another year.*

Smiling at herself because she still thought of them as
Judas trees rather than as redbuds or *Cercis siliquas-
trum* or even Judastrees, she swung the car athwart the
terrace in the manner of a pinnace crossing the T on a
great ship-of-the-line. Tires crunched on gravel as she
headed the car for the planthouse, only a hundred feet
to the left of the manse, set so as to form a broken *L*
with it.

With a glance at the state inspection sticker on the VW's windshield, she sighed. June. Poor old heap had to pass inspection next month. That meant at least two new tires, though hopefully the front set would squeak through.

Fifty bucks, she thought morosely, and she made a face.

She swung the car wide of the long building that was part lab, part greenhouse, and all love: the exhaust emissions were most definitely repugnant to its residents. She parked, with a lurch. Swinging out and giving the car door a gentle slam, she glanced back again at the house.

Three cars. The Imperial and the T-Bird—the wives of Henry Russell and T. J. Driscoll were too into their roles to think about coming to the weekly bridge game together, or in smaller cars; Henry and T.J. were making enough to afford the price of gas; what else was money for? Snapping red and somehow smart-alecky among the other two automobiles, Cele Martin's VW squareback looked just super, Judith thought. Arrogant in its smug smallness against the ruddy brick and wood of the house.

The wives of, she thought, rounding her old VW with its rust spots in the back fenders. *That's what they are. That's all they are, and all they want to be. The Wives Of. If they ever wanted to be anything else, they repressed it soon enough, for a Good Marriage!* She sighed, sure they had never had an original thought . . . or, if they had, they had swiftly stuffed it back inside the calcified mausoleums under their hairdos.

And Grace. Grace Frierson. Did she—had she ever wanted to be anything else? Was being the wife of Blaize Frierson, Ph.D., all *she* wanted and needed? No, she had to do all the proper things, play the role of well-off, well-married suburban matron—

Suddenly, as she approached the door of the sun-splashed planthouse, Judith clamped her jaws. *The wife of Blaize Frierson. God help me—that would be enough for me!*

And it was what she would never be, she was sure of that.

She stopped, a short wavy-haired brunette in jeans and knit shirt worn over nothing. *Feeling sorry for yourself won't make it happen, dummy,* she told herself. She had to get the torturous thoughts out of her mind; it was no use passing them on to those waiting inside the planthouse, tormenting them with her misery and feeling of wretchedness and futility. She concentrated, instead, on what led to the misery and the futile feeling: love. The most beautiful word in the language.

And the ugliest. No, no! Love, love, well-being, love. Oh God, how I love him . . . !

Feeling warmer, desperately in love rather than merely desperate, she came up with her key and unlocked the door. The moisture-laden heat and verdant aroma enveloped her like a great, cozy seedpod as she entered the building. Behind her, the door swung shut and the lock clicked.

She stood utterly surrounded by tall, narrow stems and short, thick stems and thin, waxy leaves and hairy, serrated leaf edges and smooth, nearly round leaves and lance- and heart-shaped leaves, and more than a dozen shades of green—along with the red and pink of the coleus and the yellowish of several of the cacti under their special u-v lamps.

She moved slowly among them. She cooed over buds and new shoots, talked maternally to them, told them how lovely they were and how hardy and healthy—and how even healthier they *would* be—how strong and happy, and how they gave her happiness just to look at them, to be among them.

"And you're all so *important,* giving me all this lovely oxygen to breathe, and you *know* I'm grateful!"

The joyously rampant philodendron—love tree—just to the left of the door was drooping here and there, and Judith paused to tell it that it was possibly overdoing.

"You have to remember your neighbors' rights," she said quietly. The Satan's-head leaves seemed to nod, but she knew it was only her breath that caused the movements. "They're territorial, too, and you're threatening violation in two directions. Remember that we love the cacti and the aurelia, too, and you can't take over their space. Besides, you're drooping, old friend, because you're shooting up and adding new leaves before you've thickened up the stalks enough to support all the weight, see? Oh, I know, you're so happy, so exuberant—and you're important and loved, too, you know that. But . . . go easy now, baby. Don't overdo."

Judith didn't bother with smock or coverall, but went to one of the plant-crowded tables along one wall and opened a drawer. She took out her old gardener's gloves of dark brown cotton: she didn't want to have to spend a half-hour, later, getting the green from under her nails. Figurative was fine, but she wasn't interested in being a *literal* green thumb! She stuck her tongue out at the grinder, turned away from it.

Humming a little, she took up the galvanized bucket and went among them again, up and down the aisles lined with flora, giving them all a bit—just a taste—of the thick-stalked, pulpy sunflowers she and Blaize had put through the grinder yesterday. She paused, put down the bucket, and ran over to flip a couple of switches. On two different screens mounted on the walls, the light-play began. Responding to her lightheartedness and to each other's delight at the nascent mulch, they emitted their mitofloral waves—which, twice transduced, were converted into light that swirled in multicolored non-patterns on the screens.

She loved to watch and *feel* the flux of the curving lines and parabolas of gold and chartreuse and fuchsia and blue, the ebb and flow and mesmeric, serpentine twisting. Sure, such things had been viewable on home TV for years and years, usually as people-holders between the end of a scene or act and the beginning of the commercial. But those squirming, too-brilliant, and overly mechanical little shows weren't created by happy plants, by what Blaize Frierson had dubbed "biolux."

I'll hook in my *plant once I've finished with the "Gross Machine,"* she mused, trying to suppress any thought of her repugnance at that next task. She had to clean the grinder. Not only did Doctor Frierson— Blaize! *Darling, oh darling Blaize!* (the show on the screens leaped and flared)—dislike "dirty" equipment, but the sunflowers were so pulpy. They left a thorough mess.

She went to it, a big metal hopper, squatting there on the bench, with fluted, twisting horizontal blades, like any household meat-grinder or slaw-maker with a severe glandular condition. The hopper of this one was ten inches in diameter, specially made by Gross Products, Inc., up in Columbus, ordered on Biotronics Research letterhead—so that its cost was ridiculous, like that of most laboratory equipment.

No need to unplug the machine; Judith had cleaned it dozens of times (*scores, thousands,* she thought, with a face). It was equipped with a simple On–Off switch. When it was on, it groaned, hummed, the blades spun, and the whole machine rattled on the bench—and crept, dammit. It was off, now.

Shoving her gloved hand into the broad, silvery pot, Doctor Blaize Frierson's assistant began cleaning the blades and the inner surface of the hopper, thinking about Blaize Frierson—but hardly as the botany Ph.D. and self-educated electronicist who was founder and, as he put it, "Sole Prop." of Biotronics Research; or as the author of several books, as well as uncounted papers and articles, on plants, on biotronics, and psibotanics; as the inventor of the Frierson Emotrizer. Judith Dahlberg, as she performed her domestic idiot-work, thought of him not even as a man, but as *her* man, and more: a sort of god—for gods and goddesses exist within the minds and hearts of those in love.

She concentrated on thoughts of him while she

cleaned the thing she called the "Gross Machine," to make the job less distasteful and faster going. Seven minutes later, when she had both arms thrust down to the elbows in the grinder, its motor came on.

Steel blades fought to spin, chewing up interfering matter that impeded their activity, serving as a clutch—though not as a brake. Judith did not scream; she couldn't. She sucked up an enormous breath with a hideous, back-of-the-mouth sound in it. That was all—that, and ever more ugly repeats and keening sounds of shock and agony. A geyser of blood, lumpy with torn skin and flesh mingled with the shredded cotton of her gloves, splashed her face on its way ceilingward.

The light-show had never been more brilliant.

2

"You think *what?*"

"You heard me, Sergeant."

McKendree Amos blinked, sighed, leaned back in the swivel chair behind his desk. His left hand moved up under his chin to tug at the skin on either side of his Adam's apple. And he stared at his visitor, his brows up, his eyes so huge and blue they looked ingenuous.

"Don't give me that sweet-boy look, Amos," she said. Switching her gaze from his face to the ID plate on his desk, she nodded at it. "That says 'Det. Sgt. McK. Amos,'" she said, pronouncing the abbreviations rather than the words they represented. "I'll bet that sweet blue-eyed look gets a lot of suspects in trouble, hmm?"

The man in the medium brown suit with the solid brown tie looked mildly surprised, then stern—as stern as was possible for that boyish face with its shallowly set eyes that were as azure as a June sky. And he tugged the skin flanking his Adam's apple.

"Fortunately you're not a suspect, huh?"

She shrugged, and under her loose-fitting print blouse, unholstered little breasts jiggled. His gaze dropped immediately to that area; just as swiftly, her hands pounced up to check the top button of her blouse. It was secure.

"I might be," she told him. "I should be. Because I think Jude's death wasn't an accident, and you should be investigating, and then I'd be a suspect, wouldn't I?"

"Sure," Amos said, not seeming to notice when his right hand picked up his pipe and began toying with it. "But I'm in a lot of trouble, right off the bat. You see through my 'boyish look' and you're obviously a genius. Because you committed what the stories call a locked-room murder."

"Maybe I sneaked in a window."

"Come on, Ms. Erwin. You think I *am* a little boy? I checked the other door, and the windows. All the windows were latched and the back door was bolted. The door she used locks automatically when it closes—which it *also* does automatically."

She cocked her head at him with a twitch of long, very straight black hair like a nun's veil. "So I didn't do it."

"Oh, but you're a suspect. My job is to figure out how you managed it without being inside with her. Like, even if you *had* been there, I can't see you forcing her hands into that hopper." He watched the young woman shudder. "Maybe you drugged her first?"

"Hey, listen . . ." she began uncomfortably.

Amos waggled the pipe at her. "Okay, Liz. I'll quit. But . . . it isn't just *why* you think your roommate was killed, see. It's how in hell it was done!"

She looked pointedly at his nameplate. "What do I call you?"

"Call me?" He had blinked and reached for his Adam's apple, and he saw her look of pleasure as she assumed she had disconcerted him by her jump-shift.

"Right." She nodded vigorously. "You're not much closer to thirty than I am, and I'll be darned if I'll call you 'Sergeant' while you call me Liz."

He made a sort of juvenile chuckling sound in his

throat, and grinned. "Oh. Sure. Call me Amos. Or McKendree. Or McKay. McKen, if you like. I just don't care for Mac: there are too many Macs in the world. Sorry, but you look like the sort of woman wants to be called 'Ms,' you know? And that sort of puts me off. It comes hard, see; I always have to *think* to say 'Miz' instead of 'Miss.' Notice my slight hesitation before I called you a woman?" He made a two-handed, rather Italian gesture. "Couple of years ago I'd have called you 'girl.' So. I learn, and I am trying. So I said Liz; is that okay?"

"Sure. Except now I can't decide among all those choices you gave me—Sergeant."

She flashed him a smile, one that looked as if she were just testing it, wasn't ready yet to go on with it.

He was staring.

"Well?" she said, cocking her head and regarding him through those goofy glasses that shouldn't have been round, because her face was.

"You came to talk. I'm listening."

Her hands checked skirt: hem tug. And blouse: button trace. "I just think she was, McKendree. Ugh, that's too long. I think she was. How could that grinder *possibly* have come on by itself?"

He shrugged. "How could anyone have done it?"

"Biotronically."

"Hmm?"

"You talked with *him?*"

"If 'him' with emphasis is Doctor Frierson—no, I didn't. He was out of town. Blows him as a suspect, right? I went out there because we investigate all fatal accidents."

"Investigate?"

He grinned. "Stop cocking your head at me. Does it put you off if I tell you you're cute?"

"*Cute?* Yes." But she looked astonished and nonplussed, not angered.

"Okay, you're not cute. I went. I found a . . . you know what I found, a bloody mess. Her hands were

. . . well, you know about her hands. She was dead in minutes, from massive shock and blood loss. She lost nearly all of it, Liz, along with her hands and wrists. The door had been locked—"

"You know that."

"I do know that. Mrs. Frierson's guests—"

"The bridge club," Liz said, lifting the right corner of her upper lip.

"—the bridge club was leaving. It was late, coming on for suppertime. Mrs. Frierson and Mrs. ahh . . . Driscoll went out to see why Ju—why Miss Dahlberg was still there. They heard a clankety-clankety noise inside, but couldn't get in and couldn't get an answer. So Mrs. Frierson was nervous, apprehensive. Something like that. She got Mrs. Driscoll to wait a minute while she ran back up to the house for the key."

He saw the lip-lift again.

Liz said, "Ms. . . . Frierson . . . does not . . . run."

He gestured that away with his unlit pipe. "She got the key, and she was hurrying. She unlocked the door. It *was* locked. She went in, and screamed—Ms. Driscoll remembered. Then *she* started inside, and she saw, and she fainted. Click, like that! She didn't scream—Ms. Frierson remembered."

Amos paused, looked curiously at the pipe in his hand, and put it down. He braced the pack on the desk with his left hand while he drew out a Winston, which he lit from one of the several matchbooks on the desk. She rewarded him with her tentative, tight little smile when he directed his smoke up and to her left, at the messy bulletin board.

"So I investigated," Amos went on. "The clankety noise was the grinder. It had vibrated its way off the shelf—or she had knocked it off, trying to jerk away—and it was still running, on the floor. The switch was on." He nodded in response to her sudden questioning look. "On. I pulled the plug. By the cord, near the socket. Instinct; I didn't touch either the On–Off switch or the plug because of the possibility of fingerprints."

"Were there any on it?"

"Didn't check, Liz. Locked door; she was alone; and she damn well had *been* alone. There was no sense playing cop, dusting for fingerprints. Something had happened. An accident—a hideous one."

She was staring, her eyes large behind the glasses, which were a very pale blue. "Yes," she whispered. "But . . . somehow . . . it wasn't an accident. She was killed, Sergeant McKendree Amos. Someone killed her—*he* killed her."

"He? Lord, you mean Frierson?"

She nodded, wearing a stubborn expression. Then she leaned forward, her narrow shoulders stiff, raised a little, and her face intense. Her hand rose to the top button of her blouse, skittered away, checked her skirt's hem on its way down.

She ought to wear pants, he thought. *And turtlenecks.*

"Yes. No listen. I know something you don't. He wasn't just her boss. Jude and Frierson were . . ."

She hesitated, or let it trail off.

It happened, in the back of his brain. *Click,* or *ding,* or whatever: the signal. Instinct—conditioning—cut in, and he heeded it. McKendree Amos went away, and his half-assed interest in Liz Erwin, born of a horn, went with him. Detective Sergeant McK. Amos took over all controls in an instant conditioned response.

"Having an affair?" he suggested, showing absolutely nothing. Except that he'd put out the cigarette, and he reached for another. Without taking his eyes off her.

She rolled large brown eyes behind the round blue lenses. "Ugh. Oh, McKay! Only people like *Ms. Frierson* have 'affairs.' Jude and Blaize were balling."

"Blaize?"

Swiftly, defensively: "That's what *she* called him. I lived with her, remember?"

"Right. And how serious was she?"

Liz sighed. "She loved him."

"Umm. And he?"

"I don't know. I doubt it. She said he said so. But that was after he came."

"Uh-huh. Did Mrs. Frierson know?"

"Jude said he said she did."

"No questions about plans, like his getting a divorce and marrying Jude, running away, anything like that?"

"Running away? *Him?* He's famous, he's one of a kind! No. And nothing about divorce, either." She made a face. "Okay, I guess it is the right word: just an 'affair.' Except that Jude loved him."

"You don't like him."

"Anyone ever call you Point-Blank Amos?"

"Uh-huh. And you don't like him?"

"I don't even know him!"

"You lived with her, remember?"

"Ouch. Okay, you're right. Of course I didn't."

"Of course. You mean because of her. She was shook up, not happy."

"The great pretender; but it was tearing her up. She was going to quit, get away, go someplace else, or—"

"When?"

Liz sighed and her shoulders, bony under the blouse, at last went down. The front of her blouse jiggled; interesting stress lines rippled into existence. He paid no attention.

"I was going to say, 'or so she said.' Since February. She couldn't. Couldn't tell him, couldn't bring herself to stop with him—making it, I mean—couldn't do anything."

He nodded. "She was in love."

"But she's been *swearing* she'd quit and go somewhere else in August, when she got her Master's. Get a teaching job, way away. California or Florida or somewhere."

"Think she would've?"

Tiredly: "I don't know."

"Um. Bad question coming up, Liz."

Her face pretended to smile. "Thanks for warning. Pop me."

"You have any interest in Judith Dahlberg?"

"Of cour—" She broke off, gazed at him. He saw her arms move, hands concealed by his desk, and knew she was tugging her skirt. "You mean like . . . lesbian?"

Amos nodded. "Yeah."

"Nope." She didn't even shake her head.

"I believe you. Got a guy, Liz Erwin?"

"None of your damned. . ."

"Right." He glanced at his cigarette, put it out. He leaned back a little, staring at her, through her. "Think she told him?"

"I don't know, McKay. She may have, but she didn't say so to me. She wasn't really weak. But she might have, without telling me; she was capable of lying, where *he* was concerned."

"When you say 'he' or 'him' you sound like an exorcist or some superstitious nut, talking about The Debbil. You think maybe Judith did tell him she . . . that she had to stop, and didn't tell you she had; lied to you about it, even. Because she got a bad answer, maybe. And then—even though he was in Philadelphia—he found a way to kill her."

Those big, almost-black eyes regarded him a long while. "Maybe."

Amos heaved a great sigh. "You came in here to tell me you think Judith Dahlberg was somehow murdered. Now you say, 'Maybe.' "

"Maybe I haven't got used to the new you."

He looked genuinely puzzled (ingenuous, boyish). "Hmm?"

"You're a cop all of a sudden."

This time it was he who almost smiled. "You came in here lookin' for one, ma'am. Just the facts. It wasn't my *body* that brought you in, was it?"

She blinked and looked down.

"Sorry," he told her.

"Me too, McKay. I just don't feel like kidding."

"Sorry I did."

"Well . . . all of a sudden I'm talking to a police detective, see, and so . . . all of a sudden I get pretty unsure, nervous about just saying 'He did it,' it's getting official and all, and so I said 'Maybe.' "

"Be damned. Now you've *really* impressed me. Now I think you really aren't grinding axes." With his left hand on the cigarette package, he stopped and gave it a stare. Then he picked up the pipe. His left hand went to his throat instead. "But you think—"

"I think Jude was killed. I mean, murdered."

"By whom?"

"How can I be sure, Sergeant? That's why I'm here. Your job's to find that out. I had to tell you what I *think*. She's dead, and she shouldn't be. I mean, twenty-five years old, three months away from her Master's, very bright, pretty, great shape, good person. She *was* a good person." She broke off a moment to get the sudden quaver out of her voice. "How can I know? Maybe he did it. Maybe *she* did—Grace. Ms. Frierson."

"Not you."

"Nope."

He chuckled. "I do like the way you say 'nope,' Liz Erwin. Ahh! Here, stop that! The button's securely buttoned. Now, we do have the problem of *how* one of them—or whoever—killed her. In a locked, uh, lab, greenhouse—"

"Planthouse. They call it a planthouse."

"Yeah, planthouse, Mrs. Frierson said that. In a locked planthouse, with an overgrown meat grinder she was cleaning."

Liz looked at him as if he belonged in a Special Ed class.

"What'd I say?" he asked, with great boyish innocence.

"You said you didn't know how they—how someone did it?"

After a few long seconds of gazing at her, Amos nodded. "I did. I should know?"

She nodded. "Sure. Where were *you* Thursday evening? Where was she? What's Frierson famous for? It was a plant. They—one of them—used a plant to kill her."

He stared, and after a long moment he drew a great breath, which he let out slowly and with noise. "A plant."

Liz Erwin nodded.

3

The man who unfolded from the dark green Mercury managed to look at once straight and un-. Though he had hardly any sideburns at all, he looked about five minutes away from being badly in need of a haircut. It was a brown and wavy mop, with the sun striking glints from it that were like bronze by firelight. His droopy mustache was sandy-red. The trousers of his dark blue suit fitted unstylishly closely, and his tie, for god's sake, was black. Solid black, swinging loose—and wide. Either he had had it eight or nine years or he'd bought it at a Goodwill store.

His shoes looked odd, without the hint of a shine; as the tall visitor came toward him, Blaize Frierson saw that the man was wearing—Hush Puppies!

At least they're dark gray, Frierson mused. Then: *It isn't that he's straight or mod or anything else. He's just unaware of his appearance; he doesn't care!* Even so, there was nothing of the Ichabod about him, though he was over six feet tall, and slender. *He's big,* Frierson realized. *Well built. In shape.*

Then the man was looking at him as he approached, and it was as if the visitor had suddenly become a boy. The face was young-looking, open, and the eyes! Sky-blue. Wide. Completely open, and . . . *ingenuous,* Frierson thought. *That's the word.*

Blaize Frierson tried to look just as open.

"Doctor Frierson?"

"Yes."

"Name's McKendree Amos, Doctor Frierson. Mc-Ken-dree Amos. I'm a cop."

Frierson's smile was automatic. "Really? You don't look like a . . . cop." *Deceptive,* Frierson mused. *Not as thin as he looks because of his height. Not as boyish as he looks because of those eyes. And he looks like anything but a policeman. He must be a—*

"Detective, Doctor Frierson," the man was saying, with a big, splashly grin. "MPD. Sergeant."

"Then I'll call you 'Sergeant.' But don't call me 'Doctor'—I'm not a physician, and I'm not on campus."

Amos tugged the skin around his Adam's apple. "I appreciate it, but I don't see how I can call you 'Mister' Frierson. Look, I'm not in the office, either. Suppose you just call me 'Sergeant,' and I'll stick with 'Doctor.' " Without waiting for a reply beyond the other man's whimsical smile, Amos looked around. "This must be the richest, greenest grass and shrubbery in Fayette County!" He nodded, looking further, expanding his chest with deep gusty breaths. "In the state, probably! Glad I got here in time to see the redbuds bloom. They only last about . . . what? Four or five days?"

"Not much longer than that. I was on my way to the planthouse, Sergeant Amos. Is that what you want to see?"

Amos faced him again with a serious expression. "I saw it last Thursday night, Doctor Frierson. It wasn't pretty, then. Yeah, I'd really love to see it."

With a nod, Frierson began walking. Amos paced him.

"Naturally you're here about Judith's death, Sergeant. What do you need?"

"Doctor Frierson . . . is it possible to talk a while? Are you busy?"

"Not really; I'm doing some things with wildflowers I've been wanting to get into for nearly a year now. I haven't even done anything about a new assistant. I

. . . think maybe I've been walking around in shock since Judith's death."

"You were in Philadelphia? Lecturing? A sort of demonstration?"

"Um-hmm." Frierson was fitting his key into the door of the long greenhouse-lab. "I was . . . being wined and dined, at the exact time Judith was . . . dying. Come in, Sergeant."

"At the exact time. *Whew!* Humid in here, but I love the smell: all green. Odd you'd remember that, the exact time."

Blaize Frierson turned around to find the detective standing beside the enormous *Dracaena massanganea* just inside the door, watching him. "Surely not 'odd,' Sergeant Amos. It's the first thing I thought of, for some reason. Seemed natural enough—still does."

"Were you in love with her, Doctor?"

That one came winging in like a change-up pitch to catch him well off his guard. But Frierson was no rookie; he answered after only several seconds of silence. "No. No, I wasn't in love with her, Amos."

"She loved you."

"You come on fast and strong, Detective Sergeant Amos. Yes, I . . . I know. It wasn't my intention that she would. But I knew she did."

"Just an affair."

Frierson met the big blue eyes for a long while. Then he took the few steps necessary to reach and flip two switches. It was with a small smile that he observed how rapidly and alertly the other man swung his head and half his body to watch the two wall screens come alive. Colored streamers of light danced and writhed like serpents. Amos swiveled his head back around far enough to question Frierson with raised brows.

"Several of the plants here show their emotions by way of those lights, Sergeant. Or, more properly put, they show their response to human emotional output. Right now I'm sending some strong impulses. You're not married?"

"No, I'm not. I was once. Does that help?"

"I doubt it. I am married, and you know I was also making love to my assistant. I told you I wasn't in love with her—but I didn't mean I didn't 'love' her."

"I understand that. It's what I meant. I think we all love the person we make it with—while we're making it, anyhow."

"That's very good, Sergeant Amos. Maybe we're about even. I surprised you by not doing the expected; you tried to see if I'd fluster and bluster. You've surprised me by being a mix, a multifaceted person rather than a thing: a detective. Or, as you said, a cop. We all tend to think in clichés, but few of us really are. Now, you said 'just an affair.' No, it wasn't quite that, either."

Amos glanced back at the screens. The lights were still there, and they still pulsed and moved. But not so frenetically. "How does this happen?" he asked at last.

Frierson accepted the truce. "What do you know about psibotanics?"

Amos grinned. "That you're it. That I'm in the planthouse of Biotronics Research, and that's you. That the tobacco companies funded you a few years back, probably because they figure your work can be of value to them, and probably for the same reason the oil companies started making concerned humanitarian noises, loudly, during the Arab embargo of '74, or '73, whichever. I've read a little. You talk to plants, and it gets results. I also know that you have plants, uh, trained, like pets."

Frierson reacted to the last words with an amused little snort; then: "All right. Plants do have what Cleve Backster calls 'primary perception.' Long before Backster, Sir Jagadis Chandra Bose said that plants have a sensitive nervous system and a varied emotional life. They were both right. Luther Burbank knew it before they did. 'The secret of improved plant breeding,' he said, 'apart from scientific knowledge, is love.' "

"Probably the secret of everything," Amos said, taking a seemingly idle step to peer between a riot of ferny things; yes, the grinder sat over there on its shelf–lab bench. "Love certainly accounts for most murders, one way or another."

"Good lord!" Frierson gave his head a swift little jerk, as if to shake off the ugliness of that concept. "Well. We're always a little slow, Sergeant, but in 1966 Cleve Backster wanted to find out how fast a plant's leaf would be affected by water poured in around the roots. It was a philodendron, like that showoff beside you. He attached galvanometer electrodes to a leaf. He's a lie detector expert, and the electrodes were attached to a polygraph. Its stylus moved: it looked like a human emotional pattern. Backster was naturally astonished. After a while, it occurred to him that, since the plant *seemed* to be showing emotional stimulation, it might respond more spectacularly if he threatened its basic well-being: if he burned a leaf." Frierson smiled and shook his head. "No one's going to burn any leaves around here," he said, and the other man knew he was talking for the flora present. "Backster didn't, either. He didn't have to: the polygraph stylus positively *jumped* . . . just at his thought. Call that the beginning—at least the beginning of scientific involvement in something some people had known for thousands of years."

Amos was nodding at the man whose hair he had decided was prematurely gray; Frierson wasn't over forty-five, but his dry, not-quite-unruly hair was almost totally white.

"I remember that story. Also about the guy who hooked his plant up to a radio beam. From over two miles away, he zapped the plant with a burst of emotion. It started his car for him."

"Paul Sauvin in New Jersey, right. Have you been boning up on my work, Sergeant Amos?"

"First name's McKendree; you can call me McKay, if you want. A little, yes. I didn't want to be *too* stupid. Living around here and not knowing about you is like never having been to Keeneland."

"Have you?" Amos shook his head, and Frierson laughed. "Neither have I!" he said, and while Amos was laughing, the botanist tried his change-up: "Why are you here, McKay?"

Amos sobered, recovered, and answered, enjoying the look of disappointment Frierson swiftly removed from his handsome face. "We investigate all accidental deaths. I need a few more things for my report—which you may need, since it was an on-the-job accident. Relatives do get ideas about suing, when they know the money's there. It was also a great chance to get into this magic place of yours and get my mind blown." Amos waved a hand in the direction of the screens. "Like, by this light show."

"I haven't forgotten your question. Back to Sauvin: he was an electronics man into psi, and connected with an engineering R&D firm. He hooked up an amplifier and a transducer to his plant. The amplifier enhanced the signal from his plant, in response to his own burst of emotion. The transducer converted it into energy that activated a radio beam. The beam started the car—and later, his model railroad trains."

"Lord. Complicated! From A to B to C to D to E to F!"

"Not really complicated, Sergeant. At any rate, I convert the energy from the 'emotional' discharge of the plants into light. I place quotation marks around 'emotional,' McKay—though inside my head, I don't."

"You believe plants do have emotions?"

"I know all living things perceive and respond." Frierson shrugged. "We could get bollixed in semantics. An atheist won't say 'soul,' so he says 'life force' or some other dodge. Sade was bitterly anti-God, but he gave all the powers people ascribe to God to 'nature'— and capitalized the word."

Amos chuckled, pushing his hand inside his jacket for a cigarette. "Sod?"

"Sade. As in Marquis de. Oh—I'm sorry, but this is

off-limits to smoking. The plants don't like it, and this is their home."

Amos nodded, said, "Oh sure," and then started laughing. "And their home is funded by the Tobacco Institute!" While the other man chuckled, he fished his pipe out of his jacket pocket. "So . . . plants may not emote as we do, but that's because we haven't invented a word for what they do."

"They perceive, and respond in a way that we call emotion when we're talking about us lords of creation. I have to plead guilty: I coined a term in a book a few years ago. I call it 'percept.' Just a dodge."

Amos looked around. "We're talking about electronics. Who hooks up your equipment?"

"I do. Yes, my doctorate's in botany. But when I became interested in—this," Frierson said, waving a hand at his domain, "I knew I had to know something about electronics. I didn't even know what a transducer was, much less what to do with it. So I sent in a coupon."

"A coupon! Really? *Off the back of a comic book?*"

Smiling, Frierson shrugged again. "Probably. I don't remember. I've been known to read comic books. And I still stay up most of the night, nearly every Saturday, watching the late-late movies. You know—the creature-feature stuff."

"My lord! LaSalle University? *You?*"

"No, it was the other one, ICS. Yeah, me. I wanted to learn, and I don't like coursework. Never did; it's pitched to the dummies. I even feel guilty driving over to campus twice a week and lecturing at UK. So I studied by mail. I still have all the books and my papers and diagrams. Got a diploma, too."

"Be damned," Amos said, wagging his shaggy head. "So you know all. So you do it all yourself."

"I do it all myself. My son calls me a psibotanicist, a word he coined. It's used, now."

"Your son. He's a . . . botanist?"

Gently stroking the leaf of an atamasco lily, the biotronicist shook his head. "Oh, no. He's not that interested in all this. Once I came up with the emotrizer, Blaize found his mission in life. He and a friend got together some money and formed a company. PSILECTRONICS makes and sells emotrizers, plus a special plant-adapted 'polygraph' and a few other things. I seldom see Blaize. He's a businessman; I'm a dreamer and a tinkerer."

If that was a gambit, false modesty fishing for a compliment, Amos wasn't biting. He was thinking about this handsome man who wore a green lab-fabric jumpsuit—with a coat of arms or something on the breast pocket—rather than a coverall or smock, and who was oh-so-cool. So he knew all about electronics. He did his own electrical hookups. He had invented the Frierson Emotrizer single-handedly. So . . . how about modifying an overgrown meat-grinder, to kill?

"You have a daughter, too."

Frierson waved a hand. "She's a housewife. Married to a high school biology teacher. A shame; she has a good mind. But I think she's happy. They live in California . . . another world."

"You'd rather she weren't 'just a housewife,' as the giggliots say on TV? But isn't that just what Mrs. Frierson is?"

Frierson chuckled. "Hardly. She has a bridge group every Thursday afternoon—she's a superb player. And garden club on Monday afternoons; she's their guiding light. She also has an excellent voice—honestly—and sings in the First Lutheran choir . . . with practice every Tuesday night. And she keeps me up on what's going on in the world. Grace reads all the current, uh, 'in' books, the kind that get reviewed everyplace, along with a lot of occult and far-out things—which all this used to be." Again, the planthouse-encompassing gesture. "Every year at Christmas, she donates a huge batch of first editions to the Lexington Public Library. No, she's a very busy woman, improving the world by being in it."

A nice phrase. And happy? Sounds like a woman all wrapped up in one man, being his wife, and trying very hard to do a few things to be important, too, Amos thought. "How about botany?"

"Well, horticulture—I mentioned the garden club. Her garden, behind the house, is a showplace. Because the plants know they're loved, of course. She also has a couple of what you call 'trained pets' in the house. But she's not involved in the planthouse; this is my work." Frierson suddenly grinned, and Amos recognized it as one of those deliberately among-us-men things. "Thank God!"

Thank God ole Grace stays the hell out, Amos mused. *I bet that light-show went apeshit when you and Judith were in here, though!*

"I'm going to have to have a cigarette pretty soon, Doctor."

"If you can't call me Frierson, my first name's Blaize. And just say the word about the cigarette; I'll join you for a smoke. Outside. I smoke twelve cigarettes a day."

"Precisely?"

Frierson nodded. "Precisely. All things in moderation. I think we should *know* what we're doing, McKay, and control it ourselves. The subconscious mind that controls most people wasn't meant to be the master."

"Which explains your figure and your health," Amos said, really itching for a cigarette, now they'd talked about them. "Do you press weights?"

"No. I do walk a mile a day, though."

Amos tugged his neck, grinning. "Precisely?"

The other man laughed. "I'm afraid so."

"Tell me about the Frierson Emotrizer."

"The concept was obvious enough. Once we knew plants could . . . do things, we wanted to 'train' them, or see if they could be trained. They can. They respond to conditioning as all living organisms do. The problem was, how do you reward an aloe or alfalfa or a jonquil, give it positive reinforcement? Backster used light. Others said give 'em a big burst of love."

"I see. Not so easy as giving Spot a bone or Junior some M&M's." Amos gazed down at the philodendron, which looked bent on taking over the entire planthouse. *To you,* he thought, *I'd say "please!"*

"Exactly. And it isn't easy, turning on big bursts of love, either. So. I reasoned that since plants pick up our emotions, we should be able to pick up theirs. I still haven't solved that one! But Swanson did find a way to record the percepts of plants, which Moore detailed in *Training Your Begonia.* So . . . I thought, and worked, and tinkered. And I came up with the Emotrizer. It's a recording of my own emotions—you know, good vibes. That made it easy to persuade plants to respond to specific tasks. When I work at night, I turn on the spotlight, just outside the door to light my way to the house. Once I'm on the porch, I 'tell' that big showoff there beside you to turn off the light. It does. But it wouldn't do it for you."

Amos regarded the out-spraying philodendron with new respect and interest. "Biggest light switch I ever saw!" Then, in a boyishly excited voice: "I'll have to see that!"

"Sure," Frierson said, with an indulgent smile.

Almost desperately, Amos played with his pipe. He was going into tobacco withdrawal. But he knew their leaving this place would be more than a change of locus. The conversational flow would have been interrupted; Frierson would be reminded of the need to get to work; and—that would be it for today. And Amos was sure Frierson would be astounded to know how much his visitor had learned—about him.

"It's as simple as that, huh?" Amos said. "Just make a record of the—what, electrical output?—of human emotions. God, it sounds like getting that first big silver cigar off Cape Kennedy and onto the moon, to me. Say, what'd you use? For the burst of good vibes, I mean."

The psibotanicist smiled, almost apologetically. He watched the tall man closely as he said, "Orgasm."

"Oh. Sure. That makes sense." Again Amos glanced at the wall screens, on which the show had subsided. Until now: the patterns surged anew, writhed, danced, pulsed, wriggled. Suddenly he thought he had it. Rather than wonder how to ask, he asked.

"With Miss Dahlberg?" He kept his gaze on the screen. Zap! Jump-writhe-surge-SURGE!

"The screens could be a sort of lie detector, couldn't they?" Doctor Blaize Frierson spoke coolly. "Except they show only response to emotion, without telling you *what* emotion. Now, I might be *angered* at your question, which was a bit rude and callous. I might be *excited*, because I'd never thought of it and wish I had— or because I did. I might be *shaken,* because you thought of it, and asked, reminding me that you're a detective who knows something few people do: about Judith and me. I knew you knew, when you asked if I was in love with her; I didn't evade or play around, you noted. I might be— But you get the point."

The air changed between them. Amos returned the other man's steady, flat gaze.

"All you're seeing, Detective Sergeant Amos, is that your question touched off an emotional surge in me, and that touched off an emotional surge in the plants 'connected' to those two screens. You have no way of knowing *what* my emotions are. Which is a weakness in the standard galvanometer polygraph . . . the lie detector. Suspects have been known to get into trouble by being *angered* by a question. One that was non-pertinent . . . or, in the other way we use the word, impertinent."

Accused and chastised, McK. Amos remained sweetly open-faced and big-blue-eyed, and he said nothing.

"Yes," Frierson continued, moving toward him, toward the door. "The recording used by me, in conditioning *my* plants, and by Judith in conditioning hers, by people, now, all over this country and in several others, particularly in

Russia, the most psi-advanced nation—and by my wife, Grace—is of my emotional response–output to orgasm. With Judith Dahlberg. And now we'll step outside for our smoke. I'll switch on the spotlight, give you a demonstration. You say the word when; I wouldn't want you to go away with the idea the light may've had a simple timer."

Amos's emotions were mixed.

But they weren't dancing on two movie screens in blue and gold and chartreuse and fuchsia, as Frierson's were.

4

For the second time that day, McKendree Amos swung the souped-up Mercury out of the tree-flanked lane and onto Versailles Road. Again he headed in toward town on full automatic, passing Bluegrass Field on the right and Keeneland on the left, then sprawling, beautifully barned Calumet—without noticing any of them.

The light had gone off a few seconds after he'd said the word, all right. A big spotlight, mounted above the planthouse door and aimed houseward: turned off by a plant. A simple bypass in the switch, Blaize Frierson had explained, enabled the philodendron + amplifier + transducer + radio beam to do their thing. He had to double-click the switch, to turn the light back on. And despite Amos's efforts, the philodendron refused to perform for him. It was a conditioned plant, responding only to the "broadcasts" from Frierson's mind.

But the swtich on the grinder was on, Amos thought. *In the On position.*

There was a lot more to Blaize Frierson than one would expect, he mused. But that was true of anyone. No one was pure cardboard. Tarzan and John Carter, Amos had decided long ago, sure must have masturbated a lot, with their women always getting stolen. But even if Burroughs were writing today, he'd be unlikely to refer to that terrible problem, the habit of regular sex, and what happened when there was no object around. Amos knew about it; he was divorced. Another writer would have complicated both character and plot by referring to it; another might well have dwelt on it.

At any rate, Blaize Frierson wasn't dusty-brained, or absentminded, or lab-smocked, or sloppy or chalk-coated, or out of touch, and he lived in *this* world, in which he was quite able to communicate. He didn't even speak with an accent—a foreign one, that is. He was a man. Highly intelligent. "With it." Proud, but apparently not hyper-egoistic, or egotistical either. Carefully in control of his life and his youthfully slender body.

And all that brain sat in his family room Saturday night–Sunday morning, just like millions of kids and fringies, watching old horror, s.f., and monster flicks—even the Japanese ones.

Could he kill?

Sure. We can all kill. We're all able and capable.

Why?

Self-defense, Amos reflected, stopping for a light without really seeing it. McKay Amos couldn't talk with Judith Dahlberg, observe her, come at her from left field. Respecting the dead was one thing; not facing facts (or seeking them) because of "respect for the *memory* of the dead" was another. *Plain stupidity,* Amos thought. And for a cop—it was criminal!

So. Maybe Judith had told Frierson she loved him, and that they had to Do Something about it; something had to give. Maybe she'd then threatened him, or just hinted that some word of their non-work activities might possibly escape her lips. People threatened, Amos knew, even when they didn't mean it. As a consequence, a lot of persons were miserable, scared, and a lot of others were . . . dead.

"I didn't mean it! I wouldn't really—" Those were too-common last words of murder victims.

Okay, Amos told himself, tooling in Maxwell. *So as-*

sume he felt he had a reason to kill her. So how'd he do it?

Simple—for Blaize Frierson. He'd put one of those little bypass gadgets into the grinder, and set it up: radio beam, transducer, plant. And—

From Philadelphia Pee-Ay? Get serious, Mac!

Then: *Mrs. Frierson?*

That had to be considered. He would have to talk with her. *Damn!* Damn that Liz Erwin! Someone appeared to have committed the perfect murder—almost.

Those thoughts had filled his brain less than a half-hour ago, the first time he'd left Frierson's place. And one thought had come back: *From Philadelphia Pee-Ay?* That had prompted him to swing the car left, drive a block, turn left again, and head back on High. His foot had got a little heavy as he drove back out Versailles Road and he waved a hand when he passed a white MPD car headed the other way. He didn't even check the mirror to see if the patrolmen had recognized him and returned the gesture, or hadn't and were coming about to pursue a really smart-aleck speeder.

Ten minutes after that, he was clonking his bony knuckles on the door of the Biotronics Research planthouse, and four minutes later he was watching Blaize Frierson, botanist *and* electronicist, open up the big grinder. Put off, the man held his lips firmly compressed and said nothing as he worked—with the switch off. And the plug pulled.

When the young-looking man under the white thatch of hair looked up, Amos saw the shock on his face, and he believed it.

"You're right. There's . . . a bypass in here."

Amos moved swiftly forward. "It could have been switched on by the old Sauvin method?"

Like an automaton: "Yes."

Seen at closer range, Frierson was shaking. Amos was actually glad the screens weren't activated. Frierson must be jolting hell out of his plants!

"Have you touched the . . . thing in there?"

"Of course."

Shit. Then there's nothing to be proven by finger-printing. Amos stood there looking into what was to him merely a confused and confusing tangle of wires and "stuff." A piece of magic called a motor, and electrical wiring, multicolored.

"Doctor Frierson, we have a problem."

The psibotanicist looked at him.

"I've got to consider the possibility that Judith Dahlberg was murdered."

"Dear . . . God."

Amos stood there thinking. "Doctor Frierson. Please don't leave town. Please don't let anyone else into this building. No one, and that includes . . . oh, a new assistant, or Miss Dahlberg's roommate, or even Mrs. Frierson. And do not remove this thing from the grinder. Just close it up, as is." *Like a surgeon who's found the horror of cancer.*

"My god. I've just become a murder suspect."

Amos had nodded. "No way around it."

And now, for the second time today, he was driving between the line of old houses flanking Maxwell, having left behind a thoroughly shaken Blaize Frierson. But there still remained problems.

I found the grinder's switch in the On position.

He thought about that. What was possible? A double system? *Install the . . . bypass thing. Deactivate the . . . whatever. Turn the grinder on, but nothing happens. Cool: it's on, but not running, because of the bypass and the other system, the radio beam activator. So. With the thing not running, anyone would assume it was off. Judith Dahlberg would have.*

The natural jump from there was to what *Judith Dahlberg did;* she shoved her hands in, and then the . . . the "thought beam," emotional surge, went forth, and the grinder started, and— Amos had an ugly vision of the bloody stumps of the girl's handless arms, and the terrible mess. He'd noticed that Frierson had carefully and surely laboriously cleaned that up. (*Odd?* McK.

Amos wondered. He had noted dark spots on some of the plants. *Otherwise . . . clean. No blood. No gore. No trace. God, what a job! And what a lot of work!*)

But he didn't make that natural jump. He was a policeman, a detective. Conclusions were to be arrived at—not, though intuition and hunches helped, to be pounced at and on. He'd just thought of a possibility, a set of possibilities. There were surely others, any of which might be what had happened, including the possibility of pure accident.

But . . . from Philadelphia Pennsylvania?

He was still chewing on that one, looking for a way around it, when he remembered, checked his watch, stopped, muttered "Gotta use the phone" to the Gulf attendant, and went inside. He used the phone.

"Liz? McKendree Amos. Listen, do you drink beer? Martinis? Old-fashioneds? Bourbon and water? Cokes? Lemonade?"

"Mind if I just spend a few seconds recovering from the unexpected call and then being blammed with all that stuff, fella?"

"Sorry. I'm a little excited. Also off-duty, as of . . . thirteen minutes ago."

She said, "I thought detectives were always on duty."

"Nah. That's just in books and movies and TV cop shows. And about twice a month," he added, truthfully. "But I'm the single guy, see? So I work weekends, and get a day and two nights off during the week. Like, tomorrow."

"Call me tomorrow," the phone said firmly into his ear. "It's after four o'clock. Nice girls don't accept dates at the last minute."

"I'll never forget that you said 'girl,' *Ms.* Erwin. Okay, here's the clincher, then. I just left Biotronics Research—Blaize Frierson."

The silence on the other end lasted perhaps six seconds. Then: "Check Box E."

"What?"

"I said check Box E," she repeated. "You must've

given me about four choices, and E would be 'All of the above.' I've been known to drink beer, bourbon, and all that other stuff you said. Where and when?"

"Umm . . . Campbell House bar as soon as possible? Or I could pick you up. I'm in Chevy Chase, or almost."

"Ye gods, you're only blocks away! You know I live on LaFayette. But I've just gotten home from campus and had a shower, and I'm not even—"

"Be right over."

"Uh-uh. You go into the Saratoga," she directed, "and get a head start, like one beer's worth, then come get me. The door's around to the side."

"Okay."

McKay hung up without wasting more time on words; she could be getting dressed. *I like her better on the phone,* he mused. *She's more comfortable. No skirt to pull down.* After standing there a moment, thinking, he nodded and turned to the attendant. "Listen, I think I've got a wobble on the right rear. Can we put 'er on the rack?"

Aside from the goofy blue-tinted specs, wrongly round on her round face, Liz Erwin wore a slick, silky-looking lavender blouse tucked into a pair of high-waisted pants, black. She was so thin that not even the unflattering Spanish style showed any pooch.

"Ye gods!" she groaned. "Navy suit and black tie! I hope no one *sees* us!"

Amos grinned, totally unaffected. "C'mon. I'm thirsty. Get a sweater or something, it's gonna get cool."

She cocked her head. "You planning on keeping me out all night?"

"No. I'm a cop. First rule: Be prepared."

"I think there's another organization with that same motto," she said, and went back into her second-floor apartment—the pants looked great from behind—without asking him in.

McKay went in. A dim room, with both its old Venetian blinds and drapes drawn. Furniture, pictures on the walls, and books and magazines were all of the same style and period: conglomerate, Early Everything. The stereo was newer; he assumed the apartment came furnished, but that the phonograph was her own. The book she was reading—there was a yellow drugstore bill tucked in, and yellow stripes from a hi-liter up to that point but not after—was an old one, Tompkins and Bird's *The Secret Life of Plants.*

"I see you're boning up," he said, when she emerged from the bedroom with a bulky blond-and-chocolate leather purse slung from a broad shoulder strap, and carrying a violet cardigan.

"Who asked you in, cop?"

"Search and seizure mission, ma'am. We have information that you're dealin'."

"The book is—was—Judith's. Fascinating. Let's go."

"Yes'm." He made sure the drugstore bill was where he'd found it. One Asp., .98, and #179356, $7.45. Page 93.

He recited that to her in the car.

"Boy, you nosy cops really remember things, don't you!"

"Yeah. Didn't mean to. Right now I'm as interested in that book as you are. C'n I borrow it?"

"Can if you're able."

He didn't groan; his mother had said that, too, in her attempts to force him into saying "May I"; it hadn't taken. "Dam' expensive prescription. You all right?"

"I'm all right, *Sergeant.*"

"I'm sorry. Case closed. How'd it go today?"

"Fine till this afternoon's lab. A senior Zo student dropped a whole culture. Not just a slide, *all* of it. It broke all over the floor. Oh boy."

"Sorry I asked."

He'd remember. She was one of those people to whom you didn't say "How are you?"—because they'd tell you.

She made a noise, breathing forcefully out her nostrils, which passed for a laugh or a chuckle. A stroke. "Me, too. It was a fine day. I told him it was *Pasteurella pestis* he'd dropped."

"Great. What's that?"

"Black plague."

Amos laughed. "You teach a lab."

"I supervise two. That's where it's at for grad student assistants. Freeing up the professors for important things, like writing papers for journals with circulations of ten. None of whom reads the articles."

He was silent for a time, heading out Lime. "You're . . . acid today, Ms. Erwin." *Can't relax,* he thought. *She's a different person, on the phone. Damn. Why do people have to be this way? I wonder if plants're comfortable with themselves and each other.*

She squared around on the seat; with pants on, there was no skirt-hem to worry about—or play with.

"Don't call me Ms. Erwin; you pronounce 'Ms.' atrociously, anyhow. It isn't the same as plain old Kentucky 'Miz' and it isn't 'Muz,' either. And I am usually acid. It's my thing. I'm still a student; that gives me a mandate to be cynical. Particularly since my best friend got killed, as horribly as in a Hammer Film. And with you telling me you've just come from Frierson, then making small talk."

He spoke to the back of the car ahead. "I'm not acid, don't like people who are, was saving the scoop about Frierson till we got into a nice, cool, dark bar with a nice, cold beer or something; and I'm sorry I called."

"Smartass cop. So turn around."

He didn't, and they talked six hours, while they shared their liking for Stroh's and then ate, and drank a little more, and liked each other and learned a few things as well, and when they got into his car they kissed, then clinched, and drove back to her apartment and got together on the couch and, after a longish period of heaving breathing, went to bed.

"The $7.45 prescription," she told him a bit later,

her eyes enormous as she looked up at him sans glasses, "is for three months' worth of the Pill. So come in."

5

When he got no response to his knocking at the planthouse door, Amos walked up to the home of red brick, redwood, and glass. He saw greenery at two windows, each plant healthy-looking and as if yearning out to the air and the sun. When he pushed the button, he heard the old-fashioned chimes inside.

Be here, Frierson. For god's sake don't have skipped!

The woman who opened the door was gray. It was not just her pinned-up hair or the white-collared, white-cuffed gray dress she wore; she was a gray person. She blinked at the tall man in the navy suit, black tie, and brown Hush Puppies.

"My name is McKendree Amos," he told her. "Doctor Frierson knows me. Is he here?"

She looked doubtful, but said, "Yes, sir. Come in, Mister . . . Amos? I'll tell Doctor Frierson you're here."

"Thank you," Amos said, entering, turning left into a living room that looked *Done,* hardly used or to be used, with chair and matching couch of white brocade, with a great shiny baby grand that seemed to command its corner of the room with pompous imperiousness, as if it had been positioned after much thought and measurement. There were other chairs, tables, and lamps; they were formal and formally positioned. The wallpaper was austere, prim. The paintings appeared to have been chosen for their colors; they "went." Even the plants here were conventional, neat, and unobtrusive. The mother-in-law's tongue must have been clipped back, or something; it was a well-curbed tongue.

He doesn't live here, Amos thought. *This is a room*

for the bridge club, and the garden club, and the choir people, and I guess the pastor. It's her room.

He remembered what she'd been wearing the other day: a pants suit, blousy at the top. She was more than a little busty, but those swells looked hard, well-gusseted, firmly holstered. He remembered her hair: done. Piled. Coiffed. Under the pants suit, a matronly body, disguised, rather than cared for or denied pampering. Under the too-much hairdo, a matron's mind; a mind that had decided to be a matron and do the things matrons did. Unlike the rest of her, it was definitely not overfed.

Poor guy. For a while, he had Judith Dahlberg. A woman as youthful as he. Now, thanks to Liz and me, he's about to have no one.

It was one of those days on which McKendree Amos wished he were a store clerk, like his father. You waited for people to come to you. And you hurt no one.

"Mister Amos? They're in the kitchen. Would you care to join them for a cup of coffee?"

Amos turned, thrusting back a great wave of sadness, the empathy he wished he didn't have. He nodded at the gray maid. "I'd love some coffee."

He followed her along a handsome Persian runner lining a spotless hallway, seeing a sudden vision of a happy young woman, every line of her thin body and face softened, like her voice; again he heard her reminding him, as he dressed, that this was his day off. But he had come up on it, after their talking and then the orgastic release that let his mind relax and think—and make quantum leaps, two. So he had left Liz, and on his day off; he didn't want to give Doctor and Mrs. Blaize Frierson any time at all.

He and his silent gray guide passed a staid dining room with stiff, erect furniture he was sure the bridge club just *loved*. He wondered if Frierson dared eat in there wearing his jumpsuit.

I'll never ask.

The kitchen was a surprise: it looked used and lived

in. In a dark gold jumpsuit, resembling all jumpsuits, with saggy crotch and device on breast pocket, Frierson sat at the breakfast bar. His feet were hooked back over the stool's rungs, and his white hair straggled loosely onto his forehead. Above him and very near his head a rope-wrapped pot was suspended from the ceiling. From it erupted long spear-shaped leaves, each with a central white stripe that split the deep green.

"Come in, McKay. Have a coffee."

Amos gave him a nod–smile–greeting, unable to call him "Blaise" but intimidated against "Doctor." He greeted the woman with the perfect beauty-shop coiffure—flash of Liz's happily mussed hair all aswirl over a pillow—the same way, but said: "Mrs. Frierson. I'm sorry I interrupted some family time."

"That's perfectly all right, Sergeant Amos. Cream and sugar?"

He'd already spotted the bottle of white tablets near the shining chromium pot, which was electric.

"A couple of those saccharins will be fine," he said. "And just a very little cream." *Big deal. Coffee with saccharin, on my day off. McKendree Amos, hero of the people.*

No, he corrected. *Of the state.*

"Actually it's milk," she was saying, as everyone did. "We don't . . . Saccharin, that's *Blaize's* trick—as if either of you two slim men had to worry about your *figure!*"

He smiled, not about to tell her he was looking after his figure now so it wouldn't be like hers, later. She wore one of the new multicolored shifts that were In this year, and even though the skirt was the absolutely worst length—just at the knees—he was surprised to see that her legs were excellent. The shift's looseness and her bosominess made her hips seem less overpadded, her gut less swollen. Grace Frierson's was a good face, high of cheekbones, handsome (that was the best word McKay knew for a face that had been pretty), and thin, almost gaunt. She hadn't always been overweight, or even plump, he saw. She'd just let go, after the children, safe and secure. (Sugar in *her* coffee!) And unwilling to do anything about it other than betray herself by commenting on his and her husband's using saccharin.

"I'm glad I didn't interrupt a late lunch," McKay said.

"Oh no, Blaize doesn't *eat* lunch, so I just grab a sandwich and salad. Can you imagine a man who eats an *apple,* and peanut butter on *brown toast* for breakfast, and not another bite until *dinner?*"

She stirred his coffee, talking without looking at him, talking about her man as if he were her son. She did look older. Because she was so standardly well-off middle-class suburban housewife, Grace Frierson with her done hair and thirty or so pounds too many looked fifty-trying-to-look-forty, while her husband—who was forty-six last December, Amos now knew—looked forty, even with the white thatch.

Grace's hair was vehemently blond-red.

"Thank you," Amos said, gingerly taking the cup and saucer; he'd have preferred a mug like Frierson's, but he supposed that wouldn't do for guests. "What's that beauty over there with the fancy clothes on?"

She smiled, half turning to the plant in the orange pot; its perfectly heart-shaped leaves were scalloped of edge and beautifully patterned in pink, dark red, and green.

"Coleus," she told him. She gave him a studied look: it was supposed to be girlish, naughty-daring. "*It's* in charge of the *porch light.*"

Amos tasted the coffee, made a happy noise, and went over to the kitchen door. Half glass. It opened onto a screened storage porch that was weirdly neat. Wearing a boyish grin, he glanced at her.

"Show me!" he said excitedly, begging.

Smiling, she turned her gaze on the coleus and he looked at the overhead light. He glanced at the plant, missing the show as a consequence; when he looked back at the light, it was on.

"Wow. Does it turn it off, too?"

"Don't be greedy," Frierson chuckled. "No; double-flip that switch on the wall beside the door, will you?"

Amos clicked the switch up. The light remained on. It went out when he returned the switch to the Off position.

But the grinder switch was on. And Mrs. Driscoll fainted.

"Could I do it?" he asked, still playing excited kid.

She shook her head, her expression now naughty-secretive. It was girlish, and her face didn't wear it well. "No, no. Neither can Blaize. That's *my* plant!"

"Conditioned only to you. Be darned. No way anyone else could make it, uh, perform, hmm?"

"Nope!"

"Well," Frierson said, getting their attention. "A *real* burst of emotion from someone else would probably get enough reaction from the coleus to activate the beam—and the light. If you . . . oh, if you were to physically attack me, for instance."

"I'll forego the test," McKay assured him.

"We have enough knowledge of flora now to know they emit different forms of emanation to different stimuli, and enough knowledge of electronics so that putting them together, we can have essentially one-person plants, like my philodendron out in the planthouse."

"Fascinating! Really far out— But there's no electrode attached to this coleus. How—"

"Sophistication," Frierson told him. "Think of a supermarket door opening at your approach, or a garage door activated from outside by a switch in the car, or a TV channel-changer."

"Oh. Look Ma, no wires."

Mrs. Frierson laughed; her husband nodded. "Exactly. With the electronic equipment I had put in here—some of it made to specs, as you can imagine, for the screens and for other experiments—we don't have to use electrodes. So we don't, much. The emanations *are* electrical, you see."

"Umm." Seeing that Frierson was lighting a cigarette, Amos happily did. Mrs. Frierson promptly offered an ashtray. China, small and delicate; for gifts and show, not for smokers. McKay coped. "Just fascinating! Do you have other personal, ah, pet plants, Miz Frierson?"

"Oh . . . um, well, I *had* one, Sergeant . . . That burn plant turned on the coffeepot every morning."

"Burn plant?"

"Aloe," the psibotanicist said.

Amos looked at the sickly, cactusy plant. Several of its leaves were definitely pallid, and the tips were curling, shriveling.

"Can't understand what's wrong with it," she sighed, touching one droopy, lance-shaped leaf. "It was fine, before . . . before Blaize went to Philadelphia last week."

Amos thought about that, staring at the plant. He felt the speeding up of his heartbeat. "Do . . . plants know about— Sure they do. Do they respond to death?"

"Of course," Frierson said.

"Your *coffee's* getting cold, Sergeant."

"I mean to human death."

"Oh, that poor *girl!*"

"Yes, McKay. But I doubt Judith's death had anything to do with Grace's plant. I still think you forgot to water it while I was out of town, dear."

"Well," she said grumpily, "maybe I *could* have . . . Poor baby." She bent maternally over the sick aloe.

Amos drank his coffee, watching her.

"Are you here to see us both, McKay, or just me?" Frierson asked, setting down his decorated pottery mug.

A little hastily?

"Well, just you, really."

Frierson slid from his stool, stretching slightly as he rose. "Then come on out to the planthouse. I've got some things cookin'."

"Right. Miz Frierson, thanks so much for the coffee. And I hope that poor little guy gets well."

The two men went out to where Blaize Frierson did live: his lab–greenhouse with its long rows of benches and leaf-flanked aisleways and humidity and aroma of green. Amos spun his wheels, small-talking, while the researcher performed what to the detective were arcane rites. The part that involved studying leaves under a microscope he understood, though he didn't ask what the other man was looking for. Frierson made some notes.

McKay didn't tell Frierson what *he* was looking for, either; nor did he appear to be looking, as he wandered about. It wasn't hidden: it sat right there in its coat of several colors, in one more pot of orange clay amid the mass of some sort of wildflowers Frierson was just beginning to study. Yes, it was identical.

"Was the cleaning of the grinder a regular routine, Blaize?"

Still bent over the microscope, Frierson didn't look around. "Once a week, on Wednesday, we brought in dead plants—killed far from here—and ground them up. They formed a treat for the rest. It isn't just soil and sun and moisture that flora must have, you know, but each other: the fertilization from the dead. Judith's first order of business when she came in the next afternoon was to distribute the treat. Next, she cleaned up the grinder. Why?"

"And Judith came in every day at three-thirty."

"Except Mondays," the biotronicist said, to the microscope. "She had an afternoon lab at the university until four on Mondays, and usually didn't get here until nearly four-thirty. And Saturdays, of course; she came in at noon on Saturdays."

"How long did the passing out of the, uh . . ."

"Call it mulch; that'll do; pre-mulch."

McKay fastened on to the familiar word. "How long did passing out the mulch take?"

Frierson half straightened. Hands on the worktable before him, he looked back over his shoulder. "About fifteen minutes. Less than twenty. It was routine work, you know."

"Sure. The cleaning up, too. How long did that take? The grinder?"

Frierson straightened and turned to face him. "Do I get a prize for answering all these questions, McKay?"

Amos didn't smile. "Am I bothering you?"

"Sure. I'm working. I'm in the middle of something new. And this is your second straight day here."

"I'm a police detective, Doctor Frierson. I investigate accidents, and murders. I'm investigating."

"Should I have a lawyer or something?"

"Hell, man! I'm not arresting you, or even accusing you. I haven't even established anything other than an accident."

"I was a long way away, McKay. And Grace was in the house—with three other women."

Amos made a gesture, but said nothing. They stared at each other along ten feet of plant-lined aisle. Then Frierson leaned his loosely draped butt against the worktable in a gesture of acceptance.

"Cleaning the grinder, as Judith constantly reminded me—she called it the 'Gross Machine'—took nearly twenty minutes."

"Nearly."

"Right at it. Call it twenty minutes. It wasn't a half-hour job, but it wasn't just fifteen minutes, either."

"Um. She came in at three-thirty, and first she passed out the things you'd ground up the day before. That took less than twenty minutes. So, by between ten and fifteen of four, then, and five after, you could have been absolutely certain Judith would have been cleaning the . . . 'Gross Machine.' "

Frierson was frowning. "I was in Philadelphia, McKay."

"I mean, generally. Assuming you knew she was here, and what time she'd arrived—that old Veedub of hers was noisy—you'd have known . . . what I just said."

With a sigh: "Yes."

Amos reached up to tug at the skin around his Adam's apple. "For fifteen minutes, she had her hands down in this thing. At a predictable time." Amos walked over to the grinder, set a hand on the rim of the broad, silvery hopper.

"What are you working on, McKay?"

"The fact that there wouldn't have to have been anything like split-second timing, even split-minute timing, for someone to turn on this grinder when Miss Dahlberg's hands were in it—by remote control."

The tall man in the navy suit turned to face the man who had to assume he was a murder suspect—and that this strangely shod detective was anything but an ingenuous boy. They looked at each other.

"I'd better tell you that I can't be a hundred percent sure of these things, Sergeant. I never paid much attention to her cleaning that thing. Think about it. Judith was competent; I didn't have to stand over her shoulder. She also disliked this particular task, a drudge-job. I made sure I was well away from her on Thursday afternoons. As a matter of fact, I usually made it my business to stay out of the planthouse until at least ten after four, that one day a week." His smile was minuscule.

"Hang around the house?" McKay glanced down at the grinder. The switch was off.

"With four women playing bridge?" Frierson waved a hand. "I messed around out in the woods, or in the garden."

"Yeah, I guess so. I guess so. Did Mrs. Frierson know?"

"Sure. She'd have liked me to wait around in the house, to show me off. You know." Frierson sighed. "Wait around. Yeah, that was it. I was chicken. I hated to see Judith do this job, but I *had* hired her, and I was damned if I'd do it!"

"I meant, did Mrs. Frierson know about you and Judith."

"Zing." Frierson pronounced elaborately, and he met

the other man's steady gaze, steadily. "Yes, Sergeant. She knew about it. She and I talked about it, but only once, months ago. We had a tacit agreement: not to talk about it. We both pretended it wasn't there."

"Umm." Amos compressed his lips. "That's common. Normal. Oh yes, the American way." He sighed. "Like murder," he muttered, then: "Blaize, did Judith have a plant—one conditioned to her?"

"She did." The other man's manner, like his lips, had become stiff. "But she only played with it, with the lights." He made a tight gesture at the wall screens. "Just watching the lights, knowing they came from her own plant, fascinated her. It was easy to disconnect everything else from the screens. She gave hers a lot of love—a ridiculous amount of love, and yes, I know that's an odd thing for *me* to say. But it's true. She . . . showered the thing with affection, as the cliché goes."

"Maternal instinct, maybe. But no tricks?"

"Just the light show."

"Blaize? What kind of plant was it?"

"An aloe."

"Burn plant."

Frierson nodded. So did Amos, who was toying with his pipe. "Hey—why's it called that?"

"Several aloes are used to make medicines, from fluid expressed from the leaves. These contain a substance that soothes burns, Sergeant. I've been going to make a detailed comparison with wheat germ oil for years. You know, Vitamin E, which a lot of us know to use as local treatment for burns, small wounds, even scars. Never got around to it."

"Isn't there a poison aloe?"

"Yes. *Aloe venenosa.* Which I don't work with."

"Poison and medicine." McKay wagged his shaggy head. "The good and the bad. Like curare. All science can help; most science can help kill."

The psibotanicist said nothing.

"*Hmp!*" Amos burst out suddenly. "It never stops

around here! This has sure been some experience, Blaize! Fas-ci-*nat*-ing! Where's Judith's burn plant?"

Frierson gave him a persimmony smile, and again gazed at the other man a while before he answered. "You know, Amos, I've gotten used to that by now. The deceptive diversion, followed by a fast hard one, right down the middle." When Amos said nothing, Frierson said: "Over there with the wildflowers." He nodded in that direction. "I expect you've noticed it."

"I expect I did. Sorry. I'm like that."

"I know. I get the impression we're playing a game this afternoon."

McKay sighed dolorously. "I've noticed one: I started calling you 'Blaize' about the same time you switched back to 'Sergeant.' I've got comfortable with you—and made you uncomfortable. But no, Doctor Frierson, I sure haven't been playing any game."

His soft pigskin shoes silent on the floor, Amos walked over to the single aloe in its pot of fired clay. He stood staring down at the unattractive little collection of stemless, out-spraying leaves, reminiscent of a cactus and yet not one.

"She gave it all that love, and look at it. Healthy and happy, flourishing. As if it didn't give a damn, didn't even know . . ."

"Amos—"

"Excuse me a minute. Got to make a phone call."

Almost leisurely, McKendree Amos walked up the green-flanked aisle, past the biotronicist, and over to the phone on the wall. Consulting a little red-covered spiral notebook on which Frierson could distinguish the word "Rexall," the detective dialed. While Frierson watched, the dark-suited man seemed to go as tense as he was. Then he was talking excitedly into the telephone, practically babbling.

"Miz Frierson! Something's happened to—something's happened out here! Come out to the plant-house. *HURRY!*"

Behind him, the humming noise started even before

he cradled the green phone. Turning, Amos joined Blaize Frierson in staring at the grinder.

It had started, all by itself.

Amos walked over to it. "The switch is off," he reported. "That may've been the cleverest part of all. Flipping the switch up to On. It took only a few seconds to do that, with the only possible witness lying in a faint."

Frierson's voice was terribly quiet. "So you figured it out, too."

"Yeah." Amos spoke without looking up from the machine that had killed—with the aid of some relatively sophisticated electronic equipment and a small, homely plant. "The perfect crime. Locked room. Victim all alone, and no way anyone could have done it. You in Philly, Miz Frierson in the house with three friends. Wow. The bypass in the grinder's motor wasn't too tough to swing; your books and notes were readily available, and I'll bet those passages are marked. First the bypass, then the linkage with the proper beam and transducer, and then the *timing*. Right in the middle of that fifteen-minute span, I'd bet."

Sucking in a deep breath, he sighed it out as he stared down at the viciously whirling blades. "The plants. Judith's is the one in the house. Has to be. I guess my word 'pet' wasn't so bad . . . like a dog, it's droopy because of the death of the source of all the love it got. But not *this* beauty. It's healthy as can be, probably glad to be out of the house and out here with friends. Sweet and innocent. A murderer. A carefully timed burst of emotion from its . . . mistress, and it started the machine that killed Judith Dahlberg: a threat to a woman's security—to her whole world."

Amos turned to face the other man, whose youth was fading visibly.

"Damn you, Amos." Frierson was almost whispering.

"I'll bet your wife knew about the recording you use in the emotrizer, Blaize. Pardon me, but that was really a stupid and callous thing to do."

"Damn you," Frierson whispered. "Oh, damn it all! I'd just got it worked out in my head. I was going to switch the plants back tonight . . . after I decided whether or not to tell Grace I knew."

"You'd have covered it up!"

"Of course. As you said, the perfect crime. Ingenious. Once again, innocent science—in the form of an innocent plant—used to kill. Damn! If she'd just had sense enough to switch them back, herself!"

"Maybe she was too scared, maybe the thought of coming in here horrified her. Guilt really hits some people hard, Blaize. And maybe she just didn't get a chance." Amos shook his head. "Remember, we talked about love, and I told you that one way or another it's the cause of most murders."

Frierson merely stared at him.

Amos walked over to tick a fingernail against the orange pot housing the aloe, which had turned out to be poison after all. Grace Frierson's aloe, which had just now responded once more to a burst of emotion from her, except that this time it had been inadvertent: her helpless reaction to a cruel phone call. This time it hadn't been intentional. Amos heaved a sigh.

"I'm sorry, Blaize."

"Call me 'Doctor Frierson.' "

Then Grace Frierson was pounding at the door, screaming her husband's name, and the two men went to meet her with the news: that her husband was fine, but that she had lost him, after all.

☆

Oceans Away

Richard S. Weinstein

1

The fourth planet from the star Alpha Centauri is a gas giant. It is slightly smaller than the planet Saturn and its atmosphere consists of the gases hydrogen, helium, ammonia, and methane. Its surface is covered with oceans of frozen ammonia. No life can live on the planet. On May 15, 2064, a maser beam melted a puddle of the ammonia.

Then this beam was transformed into a force field, which scooped up a few liters of the ammonia. It lifted the liquid several meters above the ground and held it there until the ammonia was again frozen solid. The beam then melted another puddle and again acted as a mold, to form another piece of solid matter. This process was repeated many times and with many substances until a finished machine was produced.

The machine was a c-quantum transmitter. It took the c-quantum energy fed into it by the original maser beam and returned an identical beam to the senders of the first. The machine was like a child calling home after a long journey to tell mother that it had arrived safely. It was also informing its creators back on Earth that their project was running smoothly. Without leaving the comforts of home, man had built and communicated with a machine that was light-years away.

Since the energy was c-quanta, instead of photons, it traveled faster than light. C-quantum energy has no de Broglie wavelength, so it causes no time or mass distortion; therefore, there was practically no time delay.

The men of Earth received the message almost instantly and sent another beam within a matter of minutes. This new beam melted ammonia and other substances to form parts of a second machine. Completed, the new device was different from the first. This one was a standard light-gathering telescope. By working with the first machine, the new one could send back pictures of the skies around Alpha Centauri. However, after a few quick tests, the use of the telescope was temporarily stopped. The Earthmen were too busy to study the sky yet.

The Earthmen built more machines: different types of telescopes, spectroscopes, and other sensing devices to study the space around Alpha Centauri.

The equipment's first task was a quick scan of the Alpha Centauri system, which revealed six planets circling the star. All but the one that held the humans' machines were too small to have been previously detected from Earth. The Earthmen wanted to study these planets in depth.

The sensing devices first studied the innermost planet. This world was found to be small and airless. It held little interest. The second planet, however, was very interesting. The telescope found it to be greenish-blue, dotted with many white clouds. Although the planet had no moon, its multiple star system provided the gravitational forces necessary to cause tides, which are thought to be essential to the development of life. Spectroanalysis devices found that nine-tenths of the planet's surface was covered with water. They also showed that the atmosphere was very similar to the Earth's. The infrared telescopes revealed that the planet had an average temperature of twenty-six degrees Celsius. Most interesting was the find of the radio telescopes. These picked up transmissions from the planet's surface. The transmissions were from intelligent beings.

Ray pushed the On button for his holophone, causing the ringing to stop and the face of Fred Solomon to appear as a three-dimensional image on the screen. Fred had a thin, long face which matched his tall and slim physique. With his blond hair, he was the opposite of Ray, who was dark and stocky. The two men had been good friends since their college days.

As Fred's face appeared on the screen, Ray said, "Good morning, Fred. How are you?"

"Fine. How's the new project going? You have it all running smoothly yet?"

"Yeah, we're getting there. Thanks again for helping me get my grant."

Fred was head exobiologist for the World Space Administration, the government agency that financed Ray's project. "You would have gotten it without my help," he said. "Say, how is that new assistant you were telling me about?"

"Sally? She's all right. She's intelligent and well-educated and all that, but somehow I get the feeling that she's not dedicated enough to make a good scientist."

"Oh? She's got to be dedicated to get the grades she got all through college; that is, if the transcripts you were given are correct. By the way, did you find out why she didn't go on to get her Ph.D.?"

"Yeah. That's part of the reason why I don't think she's dedicated. She said that she wasn't too happy about the lack of social life she had in college, so she decided to quit after she got her master's degree and to begin a whole new life."

"I don't see anything wrong with that. As a matter of fact, it wouldn't do *you* any harm to do some socializing, too. As far as I know, you haven't done any at all since your divorce five years ago. Why don't you ask this new assistant of yours out. The wife and I could even double-date with you, like we used to in college. It would be just like old times."

"No, that's not for me, Fred. I decided against that right after the divorce and I still haven't changed my mind. I'm just not going to get into personal sexual relationships anymore."

"I can understand your feelings, Ray, so no more on that subject. The reason I called is, I have a couple of government bigwigs who would like to look at your project."

"Already? I've just barely started. Who are they?"

"There's Admiral Alexander Vickman."

"The guy in charge of naval marine biology?"

"That's the man. And the other one is Ho-li Wong, an assistant administrator for the UN Science Foundation. He's a real strange one. He's a little guy with what I guess is a huge inferiority complex. Always uses words at least ten letters long. Anyway, I told them about your project, and they wanted to see it and talk to you. Nothing formal. Just have them in for coffee and then show them around the place. All right?"

"Sure. No problem."

"When I first heard there was intelligent life on the water planet of Alpha Centauri." Ray Morgan sipped his coffee, then continued, "I naturally assumed it would be cephalopodic in nature." He nervously ran a hand through his dark hair. Although he was a likable man, Ray was unaccustomed to dealing with people, having spent the past eight years running a small zoological station off the south Atlantic coast of Florida. "I'm a teuthologist and I've been working with octopi and squid for years. I was told the planet did not have enough land for the development of mammals, and cephalopods the only non-mammalian sea creatures in our oceans that are capable of developing intelligence."

Ho-li Wong, the UN man, seemed interested. "Could you extrapolate on that?"

"Octopi have very highly developed senses of sight, touch, and smell. They also have manipulative arms that can do just about anything human hands do. No other sea creature comes close in this respect."

"Can you produce any substantiation that you arrived at the conclusion without outside assistance?"

Ray seemed surprised by Wong's question. Seeing his surprise, Wong stopped Ray before he could say anything.

"Please don't be offended by my questioning, doctor, but the fact that the aliens are cephalopods is classified information. We have to be assured there are no security leaks."

"I understand," Ray said, not mentioning that he had already received full clearance for access to the information. "I don't have any proof. When I decided to try breeding intelligence into octopi, I immediately contacted Fred, here. I didn't tell anyone else or write anything down about it until I received authorization to begin."

Before anything more could be said, Admiral Vickman asked, "Could we tour your laboratories now, doctor?"

"Of course. Follow me."

The house they were in was built on the grounds of his zoological station. Ray led them through a room lined with books and out a back door of the small air-conditioned building.

Once they were outside, Fred remarked, "I don't know how you stand this Florida heat, Ray. This is awful."

Although he and Ray were close friends, they did not meet very frequently. Solomon lived in Washington, D.C., headquarters of the World Space Administration, so they usually communicated by holophone or by mail. In recent years, the only other contacts between them were Christmas cards.

"You get used to it. Come with me. The lab is also air-conditioned."

The building they were heading for was some hundred meters away. By the time the four men reached the door, Solomon and Wong, both down from New York, were sweating profusely. Ray and the admiral, a native Floridian, were hardly bothered. Once inside, Ray lead them to a room with an entire glass wall that was one side of a large water tank. The only other fixtures were two computer keyboards with three chairs behind them.

A woman sat at one of the consoles. Ray introduced her.

"Gentlemen, I'd like you to meet my new assistant, Sally Bowen."

Sally was a tall, attractive woman in her mid-twenties. She had dark blond hair. As Ray introduced the men to her individually, she greeted them warmly. She had been told a few days earlier about their impending visit, including the fact that the tall, silver-haired admiral was a bachelor.

To him she said, "I'm very pleased to meet you, Admiral. I read a paper of yours once. It was called 'Radiation and Its Effects on Reverse Transcription in the Squid Brain.' "

The admiral smiled. "I wrote that years ago."

"It was brilliant."

"Thank you. I'll have to talk to you about it sometime."

"I would be delighted."

Sally, obviously trying to be flirtatious, appeared merely nervous and slightly awkward. She had read the admiral's paper only the day before. Ray had mentioned it to her, and at Sally's request he had retrieved it from his old collection of scientific publications.

Ray directed the men to the chairs set up for them. He and Sally sat at the computer consoles. Ray pushed some buttons and the room became dark. The only lights were in the tank.

The tank was designed to resemble the ocean floor. It had a dirt bottom with some sea plants growing from it.

In the middle of the tank was a glass barrier, and very close to the barrier was a crab. Drugged, the crab was now motionless. As Ray pushed some more buttons, a black five-liter jar touched the top of the water in the tank. Wires lowered it very slowly to the bottom. The jar was positioned so that its lid faced the barrier between it and the crab.

A string was pulled up, opening the lid. Inside, an octopus could be seen huddled against the back of the container. Its skin was bright red: a sign that the animal was afraid.

As its eyes became accustomed to the light, the octopus grew aware of the crab just four meters away. A crab is an octopus's favorite food, and this octopus was hungry. It had not eaten in more than two days and was now at only eighty-five percent of its normal body weight. It wanted the crab, but was too frightened to go out and get it. Instead, the octopus remained in its jar, its two orange eyes protruding, intently watching the crustacean.

After five minutes the octopus began to lose its fear. Its color darkened to reddish brown, and the eight-armed creature decided to leave its lair. However, it still seemed scared and kept its arms tucked under its head to avoid getting them nipped off by some unseen creature. One arm even remained attached to the jar: the container meant safety to the octopus, so it refused to let go.

The crab was four meters away from the octopus's container, but even with its arms fully extended, the octopus spanned only three meters. It could not reach the crustacean if it held on to its container. Apparently realizing this, after a slight hesitation it released the jar and continued crawling across the bottom of the tank. All the cephalopod's attention was centered on the crab, and its skin had lost all traces of red, taking on the color of its surroundings in almost perfect camouflage. When it was merely forty centimeters from the crab, the octopus shot forth a limb to seize the crustacean—and the arm collided with the glass barrier.

The octopus stopped for a moment, frozen. It went white, and then as quickly turned to red with fear and surprise. Cautiously, it brought its two most dorsal arms forward to feel the barrier. These spread themselves out over the surface of the obstacle as if the octopus was trying to find out what it was up against. As it studied the blockade, the octopus kept changing colors, ranging over the whole spectrum. The octopus was obviously puzzled.

The barrier was a square, three meters on each side. The tank was four meters high and five across. Had it made the attempt, the octopus would have had no trouble getting around the barrier. However, it didn't try. Instead, it put its beak to the glass and tried biting its way through. When this didn't work, the octopus attempted to ram its way through. To get more leverage, the octopus curled its arms around the edges of the glass.

After a few minutes, the octopus gave up attempting to force its way through the barrier. Staying in front of the obstruction, it constantly ran its arms along the surface. But the rectangular eyes of the cephalopod never left the crab, which was beginning to move as the effects of the drug wore off.

The octopus moved with the crab, while its arms continued roving over the surface of the barrier. On the side closest to the crab, they began to curl around the edge of the glass, and suddenly an arm touched one of the crab's antennae.

The action startled both the crab and the octopus.

Before the crab had any chance to react, the octopus moved around the barrier, seized the crab with all its arms, and released a funnelful of paralyzing poison. Then, hiding the crab between its interbrachial membranes, the larger animal slowly moved back to its container, careful to avoid the barrier.

After spending ten minutes or so inside the jar, the

octopus threw out the empty, but intact, crab shell. A few buttons were pressed, the jar lid snapped shut, and lights went back on in the room outside the tank.

Ray turned to the others, beaming. He was about to ask for their opinions of the test but the admiral spoke first.

"Very impressive."

Ho-li Wong looked perplexed. "I find it difficult to comprehend your rationale. How could that fish's performance be considered impressive?"

Ray began to defend his tests. Ignoring the fact that cephalopods technically are not fish, he said, "Comparatively, this octopus did very well. The whole test took less than an hour. Most octopi take longer. Some don't get the crab at all."

Wong was mildly indignant. "Then, *all* octopuses lack intelligence. The WSA is squandering money subsidizing your endeavor."

"I assure you, Mr. Wong, the World Space Administration is not wasting its money," Fred Solomon defended his organization. He smiled, then added, "There is nothing fishy about this project."

The silence of a few seconds was ended by Admiral Vickman. "Consider," he turned to Wong, "that you are walking along and suddenly find your feet can't move. There are neural paralyzer fields that can do this. I've seen them in action. You would probably panic at first. Then you'd spend an hour trying to move away. Chances are, you would be helpless until you fell either forward or backward out of the field. An outsider could say you lacked intelligence.

Wong persisted. "If I make the assumption that a man would behave in a corresponding manner, what does this test demonstrate about intelligence, since it would also bewilder a man?"

Ray decided he should be the one to explain his project. "Actually, you're right. This test shows very little about intelligence. But it does show something. Once the octopus has touched the crab, there is a little deduction involved in realizing that if an arm can get around the barrier then the whole body only needs to follow the arm to get to the crab. Also, there is a mental synergistic leap, along with some necessary memory by which the octopus realizes that it must dodge the barrier when going back to its container. The other things the octopus did—such as biting and exploring—were merely instinctive techniques to deal with an unknown.

"But what we're trying to test for is not how *much* intelligence the octopus has, but rather its *comparative* intelligence. Before I begin my genetic engineering to develop a truly intelligent octopus, I want to start with the best animals I can find. This gives me something of a head start."

"I was under the impression that the chromosomes for intelligence haven't been mapped yet," Admiral Vickman commented.

"You're right, Admiral. We still don't know how to give the animals the genes for intelligence. Therefore, what I hope to do should not really be described as genetic engineering, but rather breeding for intelligence."

"Won't such breeding necessarily involve an inordinate amount of time?" Wong asked.

"I believe I'll be able to do it in eight to twelve years. That is, of course, with *some* genetic engineering in matters related to intelligence. Considering that octopi lay up to two hundred thousand eggs, I'll have large numbers to choose from."

"Ten years from now is the time we are scheduled to decide whether or not to communicate with the aliens, isn't it, Admiral?" Fred asked. He knew the answer, but wanted to establish the point for Wong's sake.

"That's right, assuming we have enough information by then. What genetic engineering do you intend to do, Doctor Morgan?" the admiral asked.

"First, I'll make the chromosome number tetraploid to accommodate more gene differentiation, and thereby diminish the possibility of breeding double-recessive mutants," Ray explained. Scientific jargon came naturally to him, though he realized some of it might confuse the others. He glanced toward Wong, a non-scientist, and saw that he was uncomfortable. Trying hard to keep a straight face, Ray continued: "I'll interbreed homozygous strains, thereby creating heterozygosity and consequent hybrid vigor. Through transduction I'll introduce bioluminescence so the octopi will be able to communicate better under low-light conditions. I'll greatly improve postnatal continuance of neurogenesis, which will reduce the intelligence limitation caused by the offspring's small size at parturition. I'll improve innate maternal responses to facilitate communication between generations. I'll increase the size of the cartilaginous brain case to—"

Wong interrupted. "What does all this signify?"

Ray smiled at Fred, both happily realizing that the wordy UN man had conceded he was stumped. "What it all means, Mr. Wong, is that I will use a number of procedures to make the goals of my eugenic breeding program more easily attainable."

"I see."

Wong didn't look at all happy with Ray's explanation. There was silence for a few seconds, during which Wong fidgeted in his chair.

Finally, Ray said, "It's sort of like playing the Japanese game Go. There is one objective, which the player strives for from many areas of the board. Eventually some of the areas will be connected, but all play their part in reaching the final objective."

"Thank you."

A player of the game, the admiral smiled at the mention of Go, but now he asked Ray, "What do you intend to do with your mutated animals once you've bred them?"

"I've been giving that a lot of thought," Ray replied. "I've decided that I can't put them back in the ocean without upsetting the balance of nature. These man-made mutants might develop activities on their own, over which I'd have no control. So, unfortunately, I'll have to destroy them. I wouldn't have room to keep them here." Ray shook his head. "I won't like killing them, but I'll have no choice."

"Perhaps you will, doctor," the admiral said. "The Navy would be most anxious to experiment with creatures similar to the aliens. So, if you were to give your animals to us, their lives wouldn't be wasted. That is, if you don't mind."

Ray Morgan pictured his octopi being used as targets for whatever chemical and biological weapons the navy could devise. He answered, "I'm afraid I *would* mind, Admiral. I don't believe that sharing animals among scientists is a good idea. I've found in the past that it can break up friendships as well as damage experiments. I hope *you* don't mind."

"Not at all. Just a suggestion."

Ho-li Wong began to feel that he was being excluded from the conversation. "Do you think we've seen enough, Admiral?"

"There is more I'd like to discuss, but I do have to be in Boston in three hours. Perhaps we can get together some other time, Doctor Morgan? You mentioned Go. If you like, we can get together for a game."

"My pleasure, Admiral."

The admiral continued: "It was nice meeting you, Miss Bowen. Now we'll finally let you get back to work."

Sally had watched silently throughout the test and discussion.

"Ray has Sally drowning in oceanography," Fred Solomon quipped.

Sally smiled. "I enjoyed listening to you all. I imagine that with this on-going project we'll be seeing you often in the future. Perhaps we can get together to talk about your paper, Admiral."

"Perhaps, in the future."

Ray lead the men to their aircar. As they were about to enter it he turned to Fred, saying, "Don't forget to keep me informed of any further discoveries about the aliens."

"Of course. I told you I would. I wouldn't lie to you, would I?" They both smiled. Fred continued: "My wife plays bridge on Wednesday nights, so I'm free then. How about dinner next Wednesday? I've got a couple of things I'll be able to tell you by that time. I'll call you about the details. All right?"

"Great. Be seeing you then." Ray turned to the others. "So long, gentlemen."

"Well, Sally, what do you think of the big shots we'll be working with?" he asked when he had returned to the lab.

"They seem like interesting people. Especially the admiral. I'll bet you that, right now, he's imagining himself in hand-to-tentacle combat with a giant squid. He cuts off one tentacle and two more grow in its place. But I'm sure the admiral would manage to win, somehow."

"You certainly seem to have taken an interest in him. Is there something I should know about?"

"You'll never know," Sally teased.

"He *is* rather impressive with his dress-white military uniform and his silver hair," Ray said. "He rather makes Ho-li Wong look like a ninety-seven-pound weakling when they're together; but he's no Hercules. And he's not one to be laughed at, either. He's smart and he knows his biology. He would be a formidable opponent.

"But if you want to be imaginative," Ray continued, "consider Wong. I can picture him squirming as he tries to shake 'hands' with the first octopus ambassador. Or better yet, he'd probably gloat as he introduced an octopus to the Spokesman and then watch the *Spokesman* squirm while shaking 'hands.' "

Sally smiled. "That guy's amazing. I wonder if he could possibly speak in words under five syllables long?"

"Probably not. But we outdid him when we started

talking science. Fred appreciated that. Good old Fred. He hasn't changed a bit."

"He sure makes lousy puns."

"Yeah, he almost drove me crazy with them in college, but I got even. I started ignoring his puns and that put him right up the wall. Good old Fred. I'm glad I'm seeing him again. I'll have to keep in closer contact than I have with him."

"You'll probably be seeing all of them often because of this project, including the admiral."

Sally laughed. She was teasing Ray, almost trying to make him jealous.

"You're like a schoolgirl, with your crush on him. You must have something for older men."

Sally's face turned bright red.

Over the next week Ray, with Sally's help, began his "genetic engineering." He dissected the unfertilized eggs of a female octopus. She was one of a species that produced a large number of eggs but had a very short lifespan, the females normally dying shortly after giving birth. Above these eggs, Ray released the sperm of a male from a different species of octopus, one which produced fewer eggs but a great many sperm. Furthermore, the male's species enjoyed a longer life span, with the female of the species living on to produce many clusters of eggs throughout her life.

Once the eggs were fertilized, Ray proceeded to "freeze" them. By slowly decreasing the temperature to just above the freezing point—simultaneously controlling the delicate chemical balance in the eggs' environment—he was able to keep the eggs alive without further development. This "freezing" served the dual purposes of providing "cold-shock" and giving Ray time to do other things to the eggs while they were still in the one-cell stage.

Ray used "cold-shock" to double the number of chromosomes in a small percentage of the eggs. Chromosome doubling permitted the cell to use the information from the male and the female of different species, while also providing more room on the genetic material for future mutations, including the double-recessive genes which come with inbreeding.

With the eggs frozen at the single-cell stage, Ray began preparing new genetic information. He took cells from octopi, squid, and other mollusks that happened to possess the traits he wanted: bioluminescence, continued brain development after birth, maternal instincts, and a large brain case. Then he injected these cells with viruses specifically designed to steal the genetic information of the desired traits.

He then put the viruses in contact with the frozen octopus eggs. The viruses attacked the eggs, and the information in the viruses became incorporated into the eggs' chromosomes. In this way Ray succeeded in giving the young octopus eggs new genetic information.

That accomplished, he increased the temperature for the octopus eggs, all the while controlling the chemical balances so that they began developing. Normally, the eggs would remain in the female for a period of three weeks, before being laid by the mother. During this time the eggs would pass through the mother's oviducts, where they would individually be covered with albumen and various protective membranes, to increase the chances of survival in the external environment. Since the eggs were already outside, Ray had to be a substitute mother. Using microscopic probes to move them, Ray lined the eggs up in rows in a special tank. Then he put into operation a computer program he had devised which would do to the eggs, minute by minute, precisely what would be done inside the mother herself.

As a result of his painstaking work—both in writing the computer program and in building the special tank that was under the computer's control—Ray was able to sit back and watch as the eggs developed.

The microscopic eggs were rotated, incredibly slowly, as layer upon layer of protective material was placed on them and they slowly grew larger. This process lasted for about three weeks, finally producing healthy, newly "laid" octopus eggs.

"Doctor Morgan! Come in! You had no trouble finding the place, I trust?"

"Good evening, Admiral. No, your directions were so detailed, I couldn't get lost no matter what I did. It was just a short drive across town."

"Well, that's good. I'm glad you could come. There's no better way to make friends with someone than over a game. Don't you agree, Ray? May I call you Ray?"

"Please do, uh, Admiral."

"What do you think of my home so far? Shall I show you around?"

"Why not? This is quite a place you have here."

Admiral Vickman lived in a large colonial home along the ocean front of North Miami Beach; all the houses in this strip were extremely expensive. The house was luxurious, though Ray couldn't help noticing an unlived-in quality about it. Nothing looked out of place. The chairs appeared as if they had never been sat upon. Even the thick shag carpeting had every strand standing straight up, as if it had never been walked on.

After a complete tour of the house, the admiral led Ray into a room which served as both a study and game room. Against the far wall stood a heavy wooden desk with a built-in computer terminal. The walls of the room were covered with thick wooden shelves containing books, each of which was perfectly aligned with the ones surrounding it. The books were mostly on three subjects: the military, science, and games. Ray noticed no novels—not even military ones.

In the middle of the room a long, narrow table held boards for chess, backgammon, and Go. Except for their patterns, the boards were identical. Each was made of marble. Six chairs were placed around the table, two by each board. The admiral directed Ray to one by the Go board.

Once the scientist was seated, the admiral asked,

"Now, what would you like to drink? I have some very good beer which I've just had imported from Munich. Or you can have about anything else—alcoholic or soft. Whatever you prefer."

"The beer sounds fine."

The admiral pressed a button on an intercom built into the table and ordered two steins of beer as Ray and he began the game. After a few minutes, a man in uniform entered with a tray containing two mugs, plus bowls of potato chips, pretzels, candy, and fruit.

"Thank you, seaman," the admiral said. "That will be all." The man nodded and walked out.

"The Navy provides him?" Ray asked.

"Yes. The theory is that the less time we spend cooking and cleaning for ourselves, the more time we'll have for military matters."

Ray laughed. "I'll bet it was a group of admirals or generals who came up with that theory!"

"Generals, no doubt. Were you ever in the service, Ray?"

"Yeah, I was in the Navy for two years. That was back when the UN first took over and was drafting everyone and shipping them all around the world. They had me doing research in Italy for my two-year hitch."

"You must have had your Ph.D. by that time and been an officer. Why didn't you stay on with the Navy?"

"I wanted to be doing research on my own, rather than under someone else's direction. Also, I wasn't very happy under military authority: saluting officers, wearing a uniform that you had to keep spotless, and things like that." Ray's strong dislike of military procedure was obvious.

"It's different at Annapolis," the admiral said. "There you learn why we need such discipline, and you come to appreciate it. I always felt that all officers should be graduates of a miliary academy. Any others aren't properly trained."

Ray soon noticed that he could not prevent a group

of his stones from being encircled. He began working a new strategy elsewhere on the board. Although he was having difficulty concentrating on the game and talking at the same time, the admiral apparently could do both. When Ray made his next move, the admiral said, "What do you expect the aliens to be like once we can translate their radio signals?"

"What do you mean? We know they're cephalopods from the pictures we've seen of them from space. At least, on the little land area there is, we've seen cephalopods in suits, using machines."

"Of course. What I *mean* is, do you think they'll be peaceful or not? And what do you think their technology will be like?"

"I think they'll be peaceful. I think any intelligent being would have to abhor violence. And I think their technology would have to be inferior to ours or they would know of our existence."

"I disagree. I feel they *may* be peaceful, but they may not be . . . We have no way of knowing. We can make educated guesses by analogy—presupposing convergent evolution, as you are doing in your experiment. But until we actually talk to them, we can't be sure what their temperament will be. As for their technology, there are three possibilities. They'll be ahead of us, behind us, or equal to us. Again, I feel we have no way of knowing which it will be. If they are technologically inferior, as you believe, I think we will eventually exploit them much as we exploited the American Indian—"

"I don't think so. We've—"

"Please don't interrupt, Ray. The aliens might also be our technological equals but have never tried to contact us, for any of a number of reasons. Incidentally, even if they *are* equal to us, they could have no knowledge of our presence since we're attempting to remain hidden. And if they are our equals, then I think we will eventually go to war with them over galactic expansion. I'm sure they, too, would be considering colonizing any possible habitable worlds in the galaxy and building ships which operate at near the speed of light. Therefore, it might be a good idea to attack them now, by surprise, in case they *are* our equals."

"You'd *what* . . .?"

"Let me finish," the admiral said calmly, but with a strong tone of command. "Then we can discuss the morality of my ideas."

Ray frowned, but remained silent. He was having difficulty concentrating on the game as the admiral was talking, and he needed a great deal of time to decide how to place each stone on the board. Admiral Vickman, however, placed each of his stones the moment after Ray took his turn. He rarely even hesitated in his conversation as he made each play. He was, furthermore, soundly beating Ray.

"It is also possible," the admiral continued, "that the aliens are *superior* to us technologically, in which case they probably know we are in their system but are ignoring us in the same way we ignore ants. If this is the case, they will probably continue to ignore us until we get in their way, at which point they will probably try to destroy us or control us. Or they might continue to ignore us until they decide on the best way to make use of us. Therefore, if they are our superiors, our situation is hopeless. We may as well attack in the hope that with surprise on our side we can defeat them."

Ray was becoming upset. He had never particularly liked Vickman, though he'd had no strong dislike of the man, either. But now he found he despised the admiral. Nevertheless, he managed to remain calm.

"You completely preclude the possibility of becoming friendly with the aliens, Admiral. No matter what the level of their technology, once we get to know them—and they get to know us—there won't be any necessity for war or exploitation. I believe that once we communicate with them, we should strive for a trade of arts and culture, in order to create a friendship—even if it takes ten years for a ship to travel between the two worlds."

"That's a long time for a voyage in a confined environment."

"It doesn't matter about the time. What I'm talking about is friendship and peace, as opposed to exploitation and war. This is man's first opportunity to communicate with other intelligent beings not on our planet. They should be our friends, not our enemies."

"You're an idealist, Ray. It would be nice if all your hopes came true, but they will not. We should prepare for the future with the assumption that things will not go completely as we wish . . ."

The admiral placed a stone on the board, completing a circle around a number of his opponent's stones. Ray had not been paying much attention to the game or he would not have been caught so unaware. "I don't think you have much hope left in this game, Ray. Would you like to concede defeat and play another game—chess or backgammon, perhaps?"

Ray felt completely frustrated, both by the game and by the conversation. He also felt emotionally drained, his dislike for the admiral continuously increasing. Even though he had been with the man only a short time, he wanted to get away.

"No . . . I think I had better get going."

"So soon? We will have to get together some other time, then. Let me show you to the door."

In Ray's experiments, he continued crossbreeding different species of octopi, and introducing new genetic traits into their offspring, which he also put under the computers' care. Not needed for a time, Ray was free one day to go to dinner with Fred Solomon. Since Fred lived in Washington, they had taken to meeting halfway, in a restaurant in Savannah.

The Atlantic Coast Train—actually five separate trains—circled continuously, up and down the North American East Coast, from Quebec to Miami, in its airless underground passageway. Since it never stopped, the train was able to maintain a constant speed of fif-

teen hundred kilometers per hour. Its individually pow-
ered cars, however, kept leaving and then returning to
and from the various cities along the route. A car would
normally join the train in a specific city, make one complete tour with the train, and then leave the train to return to its original ciy. In order to stop in Savannah,
Ray had to switch to the Savannah car.

When he finally arrived at his destination, he took
the rapid transit system to Otis's Restaurant, where he
and Fred had been meeting of late. After giving his
name to the headwaiter, Ray was brought to the table
where Fred was waiting.

"Ray. How are you doing? How's the experiment
going?"

"Pretty good. I've completed the genetic engineering.
Now all I have to do is wait and see how the offspring
turn out."

"A grown man like you should know how offspring
come out. You pick that up in the streets." Fred paused
for Ray's snicker—in vain—then said, "Say, how're
things between Sally and the admiral? The last time I
saw her, she seemed pretty interested in him."

"Not too good. When he called at the lab to arrange
our Go match, he talked to Sally, but apparently he was
pretty cold. It seems he's got a WAVE captain he's
thinking of marrying."

"Then I guess Sally's going to have to wave good-bye
to that relationship. By the way, how'd your game go?"

"I got clobbered."

"You? You were the college champ. What happened?"

"My mind wasn't on the game. You know how it is."

Just then the waitress came to the table. "Ah, Margaret," Fred greeted her. "Business been treating you
well, I hope?"

"About as well as can be expected, I guess. How are
you doing, Doctor Solomon? And Doctor Morgan? Do
you gentlemen know what you would like to order yet?"

"Yeah," Fred said, "I'll have the T-bone steak dinner, Russian dressing on the salad."

"And I'll have the soya steak. French dressing for me."

"Coffee later?" Ray nodded. The waitress then punched the orders up on her hand transmitter and left the two men.

Fred was smiling. "I don't understand you. We come to one of these rare restaurants that serves real meat and all you ever order are non-meat dinners. What are you, some kind of nut?"

Ray smiled. "Why should people kill animals for meat when man can make substitutes that taste just as good. I feel that if more people went into these restaurants and ordered something other than meat, we'd end the whole inhumane process."

"You're a good one to talk about killing animals. You'll be killing almost two hundred thousand octopi per litter."

"You know as well as I do that I can't let them live," Ray said glumly. "If news were to leak out that I released thousands of artificially mutated animals, I'd end up getting hung for creating a Frankenstein monster."

"You could turn them over to the Navy."

"Vickman and the rest of those military-mentality scientists would torture my octopi with whatever weapons and lethal drugs they could come up with. And the octopi are like children to me: I provide the genes for them; I see that they're nursed and hatched, and that they grow. Right now, I have a cluster of eggs that my computers are giving birth to. I'll bet, against incredible odds, that a thousand of those little devils survive. I can't let the Navy torture them. It's better if I do what has to be done—humanely. I have—"

The waitress arrived with their food, which had been arranged on her tray by the restaurant's servos. "Enjoy your meal," she said.

There were a few minutes of silence as both men ate. Eventually Ray took up the lapsed conversation.

"One of the reasons for my breeding experiments is to have man become friends with the aliens before the military destroys them. I think that might happen, anyway—the military will eventually want to wipe out the alien planet."

Fred looked puzzled. "I don't understand. Why should we want to destroy the aliens?"

"The night I played Go with the admiral, he was giving me a lot of crap. He feels that if the aliens are technologically behind, or ahead of, us then either we'll exploit them, or they'll exploit us. If we're equal, he says, then we should destroy the alien world before we get into a war over colonization!"

"Those *are* possibilities, Ray, including the idea that we may have to destroy the alien world. But that's all they are: possibilities. And we do have to consider all possibilities about what the aliens are going to be like—and what we may have to do. That's part of my job at WSA. But just because one of our options is to destroy the alien world doesn't mean we're going to pick it up."

"I know that. But the admiral talked as if he believed we would have to go to war with the aliens. When I was in the Navy, I hated it because most officers were like him. I'm sure that most *military* people *are* convinced that we must destroy the aliens. And if the military believes this, I'm sure they'll see to it that the job gets done."

Fred had stopped eating for a few minutes as he listened to his friend. Now he slowly took a sip of water, and afterward responded, "I find it hard to believe we'll ever attempt to destroy the aliens unless they make some definite military threats first. But—just in case you're right—how can your experiments prevent that?"

"If the aliens are less technologically advanced than we are, then when I have my intelligent octopi, the people of Earth will be able to see, firsthand, that they are sensitive and kind beings, not bug-eyed monsters. If the people don't *want* to exploit or destroy the aliens—and make their wishes known strongly enough!—then the military will not be able to act.

"If the aliens are technologically equal or superior to us, then perhaps my octopi can act as go-betweens in creating a bridge between the two worlds. What I mean is, *my* octopi will know we're decent beings and they'll be able to convey to the aliens the fact that we don't mean to harm them. And my octopi will be able to impress the people of Earth with the others' decency."

"That sounds reasonable. And I'll say one thing for your aliens: if it ever comes to a war between them and Earth, the octopi are certainly well armed!"

Seeing his pun ignored, Fred feigned annoyance.

"Do you or don't you want the latest information about the alien planet?" he asked Ray. "With you gabbing all night, we'll never get down to business."

Ray smiled. "Sure. What have you got?"

Fred began briefing him about the chemicals and radiation recently observed on or near Alpha Centauri Two. He also gave his opinions as to how these things might affect life on the planet. Occasionally Fred reached into his attaché case and brought forth graphs and tables illustrating what he was saying.

This serious conversation lasted well past the time when both men had finished their dinners. The waitress, however, waited until they were finished with their business before she came over.

"Did you enjoy your dinners, gentlemen?" she asked.

"Yeah, there's nothing like a good steak," Fred replied. He was teasing Ray, who pretended not to notice.

"You're right about that. Would either of you like anything else?"

Ray shook his head, as Fred said, "No, thanks."

On their way out, Fred asked, "You want to go to a pool hall or something?"

"No, thanks. I have some work to do tonight."

"You're the same as ever. All work, work, work!"

"Well, you know how it is, especially when I'm working on something I'm really interested in. You don't mind, do you, Fred?"

"No, I've got some in-laws here that I should visit, anyway. I'll call you when we get some new information. All right?"

"Sure, I'll be seeing you."

As Fred walked off, Ray started toward the nearest mass transit station. He began thinking to himself: I enjoyed that dinner. It's still a good world . . . I wonder how it is on the octopus world? If they have as many offspring as *my* octopi have, personal relationships outside the family would be pretty difficult. And a parent would have to be very strict to control one hundred thousand children. Competition would have to be awfully tough. I wonder if parents would only let the best survive. That would be almost as natural as my eugenic breeding. Everyone would be doing it to his own children . . .

I wonder how the parents would do it? he asked himself. They probably wouldn't do anything differently from what I'm going to have to do. Except I have an advantage: once my octopi grow up, I can test them as parents to see how well they bring up their offspring. Then I'll keep only the litter of the best parents.

Ray continued thinking about his experiments throughout his whole trip home. Lost in thought, he forgot to switch cars and found himself halfway up Florida's *west* coast before realizing where he was.

2

The mother octopus awoke from her drug-induced sleep and immediately became aware that her babies were missing. In the ten days since they had been hatched, she had never left them. Now they were gone. Frantically, she searched the tank in which she found herself and eventually spotted them on the other side of a glass wall. Familiar with glass, the female octopus roamed over its surface, searching with her arms for an opening to her children. There was none.

After a while, the mother seemed to realize she could not go to her babies. She sank to the floor of her tank, all the while rapidly changing colors. She was signaling her children to come to her. For a long time she stayed by the glass and watched her babies.

The baby octopi each measured less than a centimeter in length. They had big heads and short, stubby arms. Their colors were determined by only five chromatophore cells and they were too young to glow with bioluminescence. Before seeing their mother, all had been various shades of red. Now that she was within sight, they began to match the dull brown of their surroundings.

As the offspring were calmed by their mother's near-presence, some of them began to wander.

She watched them. She realized that their tank was similar to the one in which she had grown up. The far side was a wall of coral like one in which she had played and hidden from enemies. As some of the baby octopi approached the coral, the mother put on a display of colors and all ninety thousand babies huddled against the barrier, coming as close as they could to her.

The situation was calm for a while, when suddenly a small moray eel was released into the babies' side of the tank. The moray is the octopus's greatest enemy; and without their mother to protect them, the babies were helpless.

The mother saw a disturbance in her babies' tank. Normally she would have been able to smell a fish approaching, and from its scent tell what type of creature it was. But with the disturbance in another tank, all the mother could see was a form streaking around, as the eel tried to acclimate itself to its surroundings. However, when the eel began to swim more slowly, the mother octopus recognized its form. Immediately her instincts came into play. She stretched out her arms to appear at her largest, while coloring herself in constantly

changing shades of red. At the same time, she was
glowing with bioluminescence.

The young eel was smaller than she, but she would
have attacked a much larger one to protect her children.
She charged the moray, but met with the glass wall. The
eel had never before encountered a glowing octopus,
nor had it any experience with glass. It retreated to the
far side of its tank.

The baby octopi instinctively remained close to their
mother. For the time being, they were safe from harm.
Whenever the moray eel tried to get closer to them, the
mother octopus raised herself up and flashed her colors
to frighten it away. But the eel was persistent. It kept
returning to its prey, and each time it swam a little
closer to the octopi before the mother scared it away.

Eventually, the moray began picking off the babies
that were farthest from their mother. It sensed that she
would not chase it, but was still reluctant to get within
her reach. It went after one baby octopus at a time,
then retreated rapidly.

The mother octopus was becoming frantic. She made
herself look as fierce as possible and made threatening actions to the moray every time it attacked; but the beast
continued to eat her babies, one at a time. Huddling
close to their mother was no help to the babies any
longer. It made them easy prey, greatly damaging their
chances of survival.

After seeing over one hundred of her offspring eaten,
the mother seemed to come to a decision. She pressed
close to her children and again started flashing colors.
Although those colors were still reddish, some green
and blue were included. Apparently she was trying to
tell her offspring to leave her in order to find shelter on
the far side of the tank. The natural instincts of the babies told them to remain with their mother but she was
telling them to go away. Most stuck with their instincts.
Some of the babies, however, obeyed their mother and
started swimming off.

When the moray saw many of its prey approaching, it

charged, grabbing some of them before they could retreat to their mother, who again appeared menacing. The moray swam off, and the mother octopus once more huddled with her children, instructing them to leave. This time fewer of them obeyed her.

The eel again attacked the baby octopi that approached it. But this time it waited longer before chasing them. It managed to eat four of them before the mature octopus scared it back.

Most of the surviving babies returned to their mother, but three kept going, and reached the wall of coral before the eel could get to them. These three baby octopi hid in the coral and were safe.

The mother octopus did not notice that some of her children had reached safety. She saw only that she was ordering some of her babies to go to their deaths. So she stopped telling them to leave her and concentrated on scaring the eel away—to no avail. The moray was gaining courage. With every attack it came closer, picking up more babies each time.

The mother octopus again decided to persuade her children to run for safety. Several babies did run. Most of these survived, since the moray now concentrated on the large group of offspring huddling near their mother.

Eventually the green-blooded octopus became exhausted, unable to keep up with the red-blooded moray eel. Breathing rapidly through her large orange funnel, she sank to the bottom of the tank and watched as the last of her children were eaten by the eel. She was unaware that almost one hundred of them had successfully obeyed her instructions and were safely hidden in the coral. These would grow up to produce offspring of their own.

After the moray had finished its meal, a new object appeared in its tank: a net, with a plastic octopus, slightly larger than the babies, inside it. The eel came over to investigate, was snagged by the net, and removed from the tank. Then the mother octopus was removed from her tank and placed in the tank just vacated by the eel.

Upon seeing their mother, the baby octopi came out of hiding to join her. She began making a nest for herself and the babies in a cave of the coral wall, as if nothing had happened.

"We've done it! We've done it! We've done it!!" Sally Bowen was jubilant. She came over and gave her boss a big hug. When she released him, she said, still smiling, "Wow! It's hard to believe we've actually created an octopus that showed intelligence!"

"Don't look so happy, Sally," Ray admonished her. "It's not *that* great."

He felt there was somthing morally wrong with being happy after so cruel an experiment. He had come to respect Sally, and he expected more from her.

His assistant was confused. Over the past few years, she had become completely engrossed in breeding octopi; her social life while working with Ray was no better than it had been in college. Several times, she had considered quitting in order to go back to school for her Ph.D., but her involvement in the experiment kept her on the job. Now that she felt it was working, why *shouldn't* she be happy . . . ?

"But that octopus did everything we expected of it. And you've said that this experiment is perfect. It tested their communicating ability just like our experiment in which the octopi tell each other to turn on certain light bulbs to avoid shocks. It also indicated intelligence in both the mother *and* the babies. The mother had to devise a plan and the babies had to make a logical decision. So what's wrong?"

"We were torturing that poor mother octopus," Ray said, "by having her watch helplessly while most of her children were killed. I should have thought up a different experiment, even if it didn't do all that this one did. This was much too brutal."

"But we've been doing this experiment for the past

two weeks. Those tests weren't even *successful,* and you've never complained."

"That's just it. Those tests *weren't* successful. We *weren't* torturing intelligent creatures in those experiments. *They* were just dumb animals who were obeying their instincts. But this octopus was intelligent. She overcame her instincts through pure intelligence. She deserved better than she received. And consider those babies who followed their mother's instructions, set out for the far wall, and got eaten. Those were the most intelligent and most daring of the whole bunch. They might have been the very octopi that would have eventually communicated with us. They didn't deserve to die."

"But most of those who obeyed their mother *made it,*" Sally said. "The chances are that those who didn't won't be any different than those who did."

"One never knows. But don't you agree that their deaths, and their mother's treatment, was brutal?" Ray was upset that Sally displayed no compassion for his suffering creatures. He felt guilty about setting up such a cruel experiment and wanted Sally to know his guilt and share it with him, even if he had to force it upon her.

"Yes, I guess so," Sally conceded.

"Don't be so noncommittal," Ray said angrily. "Was it brutal or wasn't it?"

"Yes, it was brutal." Sally was defeated.

Ray smiled. "Good. Now that I have you agreeing with me, let's go out to celebrate the success of our experiment."

Sally had been staring at the floor. She looked up, smiling sheepishly, "Sure, boss," she said.

A few days later, as Ray went to get the morning paper out of his repro, he noticed that the machine also contained some letters for him. He punched his code number into the machine and waited a few seconds for hard copy. There were several individual messages, all from the same person; and all except the first were long.

Ray picked up the first message, a one-page note. It read:

May 17, 2069

Dear Dr. Morgan,

In the five years since Alpha Centauri Two was discovered, the Navy has done a considerable amount of work on the study of cephalopods. Considering the nature of your project, I thought you would appreciate copies of the papers from the work that has so far been completed. You will find these papers enclosed. We would appreciate a similar gesture on your part.

Sincerely,
Alexander Vickman, Admiral UNN

Ray leafed through the ten manuscripts the admiral had sent. The title of the first one read: "The Psychological Effects on *Octopus vulgaris* of Previously Unencountered Stimuli in Its Environment."

That's harmless enough, Ray thought. He found all but one of the other papers equally unobtrusive.

That title read: "A Time-Study of Radiation-Induced Mortality in *Octopus joubini*."

Damn that man! He has them bombarding octopi with radiation to see how fast they die. They're spending billions studying cephalopods and all he can give me is ten papers! And I'll bet he's got five hundred others still sitting in his office—every one having to do with killing octopi. Damn him!

Throughout that day, as Ray and Sally continued to test female octopi and their litters, Ray complained about the papers the admiral had sent. Finally, toward the end of the day, Ray said, "He's got to be kidding if he thinks I'm going to send him a paper telling him what *I'm* doing."

"You have to. The admiral will cut off your grant if you don't."

"No way. My grant's from the World Space Administration. He has no power over it. It's a civilian organization."

"He can put pressure on them, can't he?"

"So? Let him waste his time lobbying at WSA. It'll give him less time for killing octopi."

"Oh, all right." Sally gave up arguing. "Say, do you mind if I leave a little early today? I have a few things I'd like to take care of."

"I was planning to work late tonight, but I guess I can do it alone. Go ahead. I'll see you tomorrow."

That night Sally wrote a report to Admiral Vickman, telling him how much progress she and Ray had made in their experiments. The report was worded as if Ray had written it.

In breeding for intelligence, Ray mated the most intelligent families of octopi among themselves. In other words, he intentionally did a great deal of inbreeding, and such inbreeding produces animals which are smaller, weaker, and less healthy than animals which are not inbred. However, when two different strains of inbred animals are mated, the offspring display hybrid vigor. The young are bigger, stronger, and healthier than both inbred animals and normal animals. Ray had spent five years creating many inbred strains of octopi. Genetic engineering had given all these strains the traits he desired; and the strains had been selectively bred to the extent that each displayed some measure of intelligence. Now Ray and Sally began crossbreeding these inbred strains of octopi.

Ray watched as Sally selected a male octopus. Ray would have frightened the eight-armed animal into its home and then taken the home itself and put it into the female's tank. Octopi, however, are nervous animals; and if frightened, they may not mate. Sally, therefore, transferred the octopus cautiously.

She put her right arm into the octopus's tank and held her arm there, keeping it very still. At the sight of the human arm, the cephalopod anchored its two most rear, or ventral, arms on a solid rock. Then, after a minute or two, it brought one of its most dorsal arms to Sally's hands and touched it. The octopus's arm next curled around the hand while the suckers studied it.

Sally now put her left hand into the tank, moving the fingers of that hand to interest the octopus. But Sally kept her left hand out of the octopus's reach as long as it remained attached to the rock. The octopus by now had faith in the solidity of Sally's right arm. Therefore, it released the rock and used Sally's appendage as an anchor. Then it brought one of its arms up to Sally's left hand in order to study it.

She kept both her arms in the tank for a while to let the octopus become comfortable. Finally, keeping her right arm as stiff as possible, she slowly lifted the octopus from the tank. Octopi can remain out of water for up to twenty minutes as long as they are kept moist. Some species purposely leave the water to hunt crabs on beaches and rocks. For that reason, the octopus was not unduly alarmed at leaving the water. It clung to Sally's arms.

Sally talked to the octopus as she carried it to the female's tank. "It's all right, old fella. Don't be scared. This is your big day." She stroked the octopus with the fingers of her left hand.

Carrying the octopus to its mate's tank, she lowered it into the water. She let it anchor itself to a rock in the tank. Then she shook its arms off her own and pulled her arms out of the water.

Ray watched as Sally worked. He was moved by the care and the feeling she displayed toward his creatures; she had a patience he did not have with them. And she talked to them when she knew they could not hear her. Ray told himself he must not say anything to her: Sally was a scientist and everything she did was logical. It was better for the octopi if she seemed to care. And she just naturally had more patience than he did. Also, the octopus could sense—just from the vibrations of her voice and the attitude that her own talking created in *her*—that it need not be afraid. Sally was being purely scientific, Ray tried to convince himself.

The female octopus watched from her home as the male was placed in her tank. Now she inched out and began a thorough cleaning of her sucker disks. She was making an obvious action of displaying her suckers to the male.

The male responded by displaying his sucker disks, too. He had one disk much larger than the rest—this large disk a distinguishing characteristic of all male octopi.

The female started glowing faintly.

The male's eyes widened. He was intent only upon his mate. The rings around his eyes darkened, and then he started to glow brightly. He was soon much brighter than the female.

He started crawling across the bottom of the tank toward the female. When his arms were almost touching hers, he shot above her in one jet-like burst. Then he slowly sank on top of her, in his excitement changing colors constantly. He seized her by the head with his two most dorsal arms; then he surrounded her with his interbrachial membrane. He was protecting her in case they should be attacked while mating. At such times, octopi are oblivious to anything that happens in their surroundings.

The female octopus raised her dorsal arms over the male and held him by his head. All her other arms were rolled up. The male rolled up his arms too—all except the two with which he held her, and one other arm. This arm, the third from the right of his head, is called the hectocotylus. The hectocotylized arm is different from the others: it has a groove which runs between the suckers, from the tip of the arm to its base. In addition, the tip of the arm widens slightly and flattens out. The hectocotylus is the male octopus's copulatory organ.

The male now used this strange arm to caress the female. Keeping it under him, he ran it over her body. Finally, he inserted it into her body cavity.

The hectocotylized arm spasmed for a few seconds and then stopped. The spasms returned every ten minutes for the next hour, forcing large sperm sacks, or spermatophores, along the groove of the arm and into the female.

Eventually the female pushed the male off, and he crawled away as she crawled back to her home.

Sally now put her arms into the tank and picked up the male octopus. This time he did not try to hold to any rocks. He came away freely. Sally petted and talked to the octopus as she carried him back to his home.

Sally then went across to the sink to wash the saltwater from her arms. As she did, she said to Ray, "You're going to work late tonight?"

"Yeah, I've got some planning to do for some new experiments."

"Do you want me to stay?"

"No, you can go . . ."

"You want me to make some coffee, or go get some dinner and bring it back?"

"No. I'll get something for myself later. Thanks for asking."

Sally said good night and took the lonely walk out to the Metro station.

A few weeks later, Ray was preparing for a new experiment as Sally arrived in the lab.

"Good morning, boss," she said.

He looked up. "Hi. How'd your singles party go last night?"

"Awful. Half the people there thought only, and constantly, about sex."

"Well, that's what they were there for."

"I know, but I expected some conversation and dancing and things, first."

"And there wasn't any?"

"Oh, some. But the conversations tended to be esoteric discussions about some Russian dancer, or sports, or about novels I haven't read. The one conversation I knew anything about started with a guy complaining about a fusion plant going up in his neighborhood. Most of the people didn't even know the difference between fusion and fission. It was horrible. They were all idiots."

"Well, you've studied science all your life and they've studied Russian dancers. That's the problem."

"You should have come with me. At least the two of us could have stood around and laughed at them all."

"I was busy getting things set up for this new experiment today. I stayed awake half the night setting things up after the equipment came in last evening."

Ray looked bleary-eyed, his hair was uncombed, and his shirt and slacks were full of wrinkles.

"You should go out and relax more, boss. Or at least get some sleep. It looks like you've been sleeping in those clothes for the past two weeks. You're going to get yourself sick, if you don't take a rest."

"I've been anxious to get started on this experiment," Ray answered in a defensive, almost bitter, tone. "And besides, the admiral has a few billion dollars and thousands of people working for him. I've got to work hard to keep up."

Ray was trying to be funny, but Sally didn't see the humor. "You're going to kill yourself. You can't keep working this way. Why don't you take the day off and get some sleep?"

"Don't tell me what to do!" Ray shouted. He was angry at Sally for caring for him, and for going to singles parties—and imagining him there with her. Also he truly felt the military was pressing him for time. "I've got to finish this thing before the admiral and his friends destroy the aliens. Get that through your head."

Sally was surprised and confused. "Well, if that's the way you feel about it, I'll . . . I'll—"

"I'm sorry, Sally. I don't know what got into me. I've got a short temper when I'm tired. Forgive me?"

Sally looked up. She had a peculiar smile on her face which told that she didn't quite understand what had happened but was glad it was over. "Sure, boss."

"Let's get to work. Okay?"

She nodded.

"Good," Ray said. "I've finally gotten our communications board interfaced with the computer and ready to go. I was just about to try it out with the first octopus when you came in. I'll let him demonstrate it for you. All right?"

"Fine."

Sally was staring at the communications board inside the octopus tank. She slid into her seat as Ray turned out all the lights except a few dim ones in the tank.

An open octopus jar was then lowered into the tank. The jar was made to turn upside down, and the octopus floated out. The jar was then removed from the tank.

The octopus was a fairly large male, nearly four meters in diameter and twelve kilograms in weight. The large head between its bulging eyes caused the octopus's body to appear small. Since it was accustomed to being moved from one tank to another, the octopus was its normal purplish-gray color.

As it became acclimated to its new surroundings, the octopus noticed the lighted communications board on one wall of the tank. The cephalopod floated to the bottom of the tank, then crawled along the bottom to the board—a square, three meters to a side, with one hundred buttons, some of which contained pictures.

Although all the buttons were lighted, one was brighter than the others. It was to this button that the octopus was attracted. The cephalopod brought forth an arm to touch the bright object, the tip of the arm encircling the button; but the octopus applied no pressure to it: he was exploring.

When its curiosity about the lighted button was satisfied, the octopus attempted to move along the board. In moving, the cephalopod pushed off from the lighted button. Feeling the button move as he pushed, he immediately released it. But too late. Pushing the button had caused all the lights to go on in the tank.

The octopus moved in a rocket-like burst of speed toward the center of the tank, leaving a deep purple cloud where it had been. Its skin, which had suddenly gone white with shock, now changed to red. The eight-armed animal again sank to the bottom of the tank, studying the communications board to see if it made any threatening actions.

When, after some time, the board remained inanimate, the octopus regained its normal color and slowly crept over to it again. This time the octopus avoided the brightly lit button as it studied the others. One button had the drawing of a crab on it. It was to this button that the octopus now directed its attention.

As it had done with the lighted button, the octopus encircled the button with the tip of one arm; and while trying to move, the octopus once more inadvertently pushed the button. But this time a small door on the wall of the communication panel opened, to reveal a live crab. As the crab proceeded to crawl out of its confined quarters, the octopus seized it, poisoned it, and carried it to a corner of the tank.

Here, while it continued trying to hide the crab between its interbrachial membrane, the octopus used two arms to bend the crustacean in order to widen the natural cracks in the shell and inserted the very small ends of its other arms into these cracks to pull out the meat of the crab and bring the food to its mouth.

Once done with its meal, the male octopus again returned to the communication panel. He put one arm on the button with the crab drawing and deliberately pushed it. The small door again opened and another crab came out. Having just finished a meal, the octopus left this crab unmolested. Instead, the octopus continued pushing buttons, being rewarded with whatever was drawn on the button. Buttons without drawings produced nothing. Nevertheless, the octopus managed to fill its tank with jars, rocks, and many species of fish which octopi consider food.

The octopus had now turned an orange color and had ridges over its eyes—for an octopus, signs of happiness.

"Well, what do you think of that?" Ray Morgan asked.

"Interesting," Sally replied. "It gets the octopus to equate pictures with objects."

"Right. Once the octopus gets used to what all the basic buttons mean, I'll stick in some new buttons that mean 'Give' and 'Take,' 'Turn on' and 'Turn off.' Then, if the octopus wants a crab it'll press the buttons 'Give' and 'Crab' in that order. After doing it by random chance a few times, the octopus will learn what it *has* to do. Once it learns these fairly simple things, I can continue making the sequence more complicated until the octopus is finally putting together sentences like: 'Computer, please give crab.' "

"Ever since you first told me about this experiment, I've been wondering if you've really established communication? I mean, it's just memory—learning by rote."

"The octopus probably starts out memorizing what button combinations mean what; but eventually it comes out with language. At least it has in the past. As I've told you before, this experiment was done a long time ago with chimpanzees. You give them a new word and they know how to use it in a sentence. For example, if a chimp's been taught how to use the word 'window' and you give it the word 'door,' it will know to use the words 'open' and 'close' with 'door.' You won't find the chimp saying 'Give door,' or 'Turn on door.' The chimp knows the relationship between the words 'door' and 'window' and also knows the relationship between 'open' and 'window.' That's an understanding of language, not just memory. Hopefully, the same thing will happen with my octopi."

"And you can talk to the octopus with your panel?"

"That's right."

They both looked to Ray's left at a smaller version of the panel that was in the octopus tank. Ray's panel was one meter square, covered with buttons, and lying flat on an extension of Ray's desk. "Whenever I press one of my buttons it causes a red light to go on in the corresponding button in the octopus's panel. Watch."

Ray pressed a button that had a lobster drawn on it. This action caused the corresponding button to light up red in the octopus tank, while a small door opened and a lobster was pushed out. The octopus, which had retired to a jar in the tank, remained unaware of any action.

"So what you're doing," Sally elaborated, thinking about each word as she said it, "is creating a new computer language, which *you* learn, and the *octopus* has to learn, so that both of you can communicate with the computer. You're communicating with each other, only indirectly."

"What's wrong with that? This way *I* don't have to watch the octopus all the time. The computer is teaching the octopus even when I'm not around."

"There's nothing wrong with it, *per se*. But why do you have to teach the octopus a new language? We can use the one it already has."

Sally had a gleam in her eyes. Even though she was talking, she gave the appearance of being lost in thought as she worked out the methods for her idea.

"And how do you intend to do that?" Ray asked smugly.

In attempting to control his own feelings for Sally, he had begun thinking of her as part of the machinery necessary to keep the experiment going. He found he resented the fact that she was trying to act as an equal partner, creating her own experiments.

"We know a lot of reactions an octopus has, to certain emotions: red for fear, orange for happiness, white for shock, and a bunch of others. I'm sure I could reproduce them. I took a lot of art courses in college. I'm a good artist."

"How do you propose we use your art? Do we put one of your paintings in the water every time we want to talk to an octopus?"

"I could have them made into slides so we could show them on a wall of the tank and change them quickly."

"That brings up another point," Ray said. "Half of their reactions have to do with *how* they change their colors, not just the colors they change to. With your slide idea, we'd be cutting out a lot of their 'words.' "

"Well then, we can . . . uh . . . animate the drawings, like an animated cartoon."

"Right, then we 'd have an Oswald the Octopus cartoon. And every Saturday afternoon we could invite the neighbor's kids in for a matinee showing."

"Come on, Ray. Be fair. It's as good as *your* idea."

"Now look," Ray said, somewhat annoyed. "My idea's been tried before and it works. The closest anyone's come to what you have in mind is when they tried sending porpoise signals back at a porpoise. All that did was confuse the porpoise. If we were to switch over to your system it would waste time even if your system worked, and if it didn't work we'd be wasting more time. Time is most important to me. In case you've forgotten already, I'm trying to finish this thing before the military destroys that planet.

"But, Ray, don't condemn something just because it's new. It's probably better: you'll save time in not having to teach each octopus your new language. And communicating with the aliens will be lot easier, if you already know something about how a cephalopod communicates."

"Will you stop arguing, damnit!" Ray shouted. "If you want to meddle in somebody's experiment, get your own. I'm the one who's running this one and it's going to be done the way I want it to be done."

"Well, all right. I was just trying to help. You asked my opinion and . . ."

Ray glared at Sally and she stopped talking immediately. The rest of the day went by in near-silence.

The next morning, when Sally came to work, Ray said, "Hi. I . . . did a lot of thinking last night, and decided you weren't so dumb after all."

"What?" she asked, smiling.

"Your method of communicating with the octopi through animated drawings—I've decided to try it. I called the computer company this morning to order a hologram tank to reproduce drawings in three dimensions. It's your idea but in 3-D."

"Hey, that's great. And you won't be sorry, Ray. It'll work! I'm *sure* it will."

"If it doesn't, you're in big trouble."

"You wouldn't blame little old me?"

Ray laughed. "No, I'll only turn you over my knee and spank you."

Sally blushed. "And what will you do . . . if it works?"

Ray turned suddenly serious. He sensed that Sally was hinting at an action more intimate than spanking. "We'll see about that when we come to it," he said. Then, hesitating for a few seconds, he continued: "Sally, my decision to use your idea was only a part of what I thought about last night. There are some things I think we should talk about . . ."

"Oh?"

"Not here. They're not about work, really, but things we should straighten out between us. Are you free for dinner tonight? I mean, uh, so we can talk then."

Ray was trying hard to make certain his invitation to dinner did not sound as if it were a prelude to the more intimate relationship Sally wanted.

"Well, yeah, sure, Ray. That would be fine."

"Would either of you care for a cocktail?" the waiter asked.

Ray looked toward Sally.

"No. No, thank you." She rarely had occasions for social drinking in her life. And on those few times she did drink, she found she didn't like it.

The waiter glanced at Ray and was about to leave, when Ray said, "Hmmm," frowning. "I'll have a martini, anyway; extra dry and no ice."

"If you're getting something, I guess I should have something too . . ."

"What would you like?"

Sally paused as she ran through her memory for the name of a drink. Finally, she said the first name that popped into her head, hoping it had stuck in her memory because she liked it, rather than because she'd found it distasteful. "I'll have a brandy Alexander."

Once the waiter had left, she said, "I didn't know that you drink."

Ray smiled at Sally's innocence. He realized now why she had paused before coming up with the name of a drink.

"Back in college days, Fred and I had to carry each other out of some of the places we went to. It was always a great way to relax and forget about work. Schoolwork, in those days . . . But drinking also helps to loosen the tongue a bit."

He was sorry about the last sentence as soon as he said it. Sally now expected him to say why he invited her to dinner, but he wasn't ready yet. The drinks arrived and he took a big gulp of his martini but still remained silent, looking out the window at two seagulls that were flying in the same direction over Biscayne Bay. They seemed not to notice each other. Ray wished he were there with them.

After a few seconds, Sally realized what was happening and tried to keep the conversation going. "You and Fred were really close in those days, weren't you?"

"Yes. We roomed together, and we were studying pretty much the same things, so we were always helping each other out. Then, on the weekends, we'd unwind together. He's probably the best friend I've ever had."

The conversation ended for a while, and Ray used the time to finish off his drink. Sally, seeing Ray done with his, finished her cocktail also. Ray managed to catch the waiter's eye and ordered another round. When the new drinks came, he took one sip and said, "Sally, I'm under the opinion that you . . . No. That's no way to start."

He sipped his drink again and began, "Sally, have you ever wondered why my, uh, ex-wife and I are divorced?"

"That happened long before I met you and I always thought you wouldn't want me to bring it up."

"You're probably right, but now I'm going to tell you. At the time I met my wife, I was working on the research project for my Ph.D. I had a really superb project on the nerve physiology of the squid. It could have been one of the important works on research of the brain . . .

"My mentor jokingly suggested that I might win the Nobel Prize with that paper, and I used to dream of it. Realistically, though, I just hoped to get a name in the field before I even got into it.

"My professor was Dr. James Berenson. He was brilliant. But he was never dedicated enough in research to make a name for himself. He was *very* dedicated to his students, though, and he and I were very close. I think he expected me to be one student who really did something important."

Ray stopped, took a sip of his drink, and said, "Here I am, telling you all about my life and that's not what I wanted to talk to you about. I guess I'm trying to avoid the subject again."

"That's all right," Sally said. "I'm interested. Keep going."

Ray took a sip from his martini and continued: "I was just beginning my Ph.D. research when I met Denise—my ex-wife. Fred and I, and some of our friends, were invited to a party and I found her there, talking to another girl about a novel that I happened to have read.

We hit it off well together, and pretty soon I was with her almost constantly. I began to neglect my work, especially my research project. But I didn't care. From the night I met Denise until we were married was the happiest time of my life. I'm sure I had a shine in my eyes in those years and I was healthier than I've ever been. I truly enjoyed living."

The setting sun in the window gave Ray's face golden highlights. Sally thought his gray eyes seemed incredibly clear and intelligent. She was about to say something, but then decided it would be better to let Ray tell his story without any interference from her.

Ray was still talking. "But I wasn't doing much work. I began to modify my project so I could spend more time with Denise, and what work I did I rushed through. Dr. Berensen was unbelievably nice about it. He liked me and saw that I was happy. He didn't want to interfere with my happiness. And he knew that I would get my degree, with a paper which was one-tenth as good as the one I had started out on. Now that I think back on it, I guess it would have been better in the long run if Dr. Berenson had insisted I continue with my original thesis.

"As it was, I did manage to get my degree, but I couldn't even get my paper published. It didn't matter much at the time because I was drafted into the Navy as an officer and on my salary, I was able to marry Denise and live comfortably. I think there was something wrong with our marriage even then, but I blamed all my problems on the military.

"I despised military life. They had me saluting officers who ware complete idiots. Then they shipped us out to a base in Italy. I always had to keep my shoes polished and my uniform spotless, or I'd get a reprimand. In addition, I was doing research under someone else's direction. I hated it.

"When I got out of the navy, Fred offered to get me a job with the WSA but I refused to work for the government again. Instead, I applied for a grant to start my own research station here in Florida. I got it and we moved; but soon Denise was complaining that I was spending too much time working and not enough with her. She was right, but the novelty had worn out of our marriage by that time, and I was fascinated with my work.

"For the first time since I'd met her, I was truly interested in the research I was doing; and I felt it was important. But whenever I spent extra time in the laboratory, she got angry with me. And every weekend, she nagged me to do something with her—because she couldn't excuse my working on weekends. I was always feeling guilty because I neglected her.

"Pretty soon I found myself spending more and more time working, just to avoid Denise. The situation continued for a few years, with both of us miserable. Then, one day, she really got angry and started throwing things. I threw them back and our marriage was over. We agreed on a divorce and that was that.

"So, do you see, Sally, why I don't want *our* relationship to go beyond that of an employer and employee?"

Sally did not look very happy, but she was not surprised by what Ray had said. She had known all along that he was deliberately being distant with her; and as soon as he mentioned his wife, she realized that he was trying to give her the reason. She tried to make her voice seem sincere, but somehow it came out sounding cold and uncaring.

"No," she said. "I mean, I'm sorry that your marriage didn't work out. And I think I understand that you're afraid too much of a social life would interfere with your work. But I don't understand how all this pertains to me. After all, I'm part of your *work*. I'm working on this project with you."

"I'm not afraid of a social life, at all. I believe in playing cards and doing things with some friends whenever my work gives me some spare time. But I've come to realize that you're, well, interested in a . . . a deeper relationship than you've had with me. *That's* what I'm afraid of—of getting involved to the extent that my work becomes unimportant to me. I think my work would be much better off—and you and me too, I guess—if we just stayed at the employer-employee level."

Ray was not sure Sally accepted his opinion, or just accepted the fact that she could not change his mind. She remained quiet and began eating her dinner, which had just arrived. Ray also started, as the waiter poured wine.

Sally now felt she understood why Ray was being distant toward her. She sympathized with him, though she was intent on changing his mind; but she realized that nothing she could say now would have an effect. As she ate, she became despondent, concluding that she would never be able to get Ray to appreciate her.

They ate for a while in silence. As they did, Ray glanced over at his assistant. The sun setting behind her made her dark blond hair glisten like gold, giving her softly curved face an almost angelic appearance. The effect was heightened by the redness of her cheeks. Ray looked at the bottle of wine on the table and decided that Sally had drunk much more than he had. The wine, and the two cocktails earlier, had probably caused the flush. But he felt that the pink suited her. He also noticed a faint trace of tears in her eyes. Caused by the alcohol too, I hope, he told himself.

After a while, Sally began to speak. "All my life . . . from elementary school to gradaute school . . . I worked really hard to achieve perfect grades. I don't think I've ever received anything less than perfect. I don't know *why* I worked so hard; I imagine that originally it was to please my parents. But in studying so much, I never made an effort to look good or to socialize.

"Most of the boys shied away from me and I never tried to flirt with them. I had little interest in the few who did ask me out. On the small number of dates I had, I never could bring myself to say yes when they asked me for a second date. I still don't know why. I've thought that I did because I dreamed of being asked out by some other boy who didn't even know I existed. I used to cry about it after a date, when I said no. I always used to tell myself that I would say yes the next time, but knew I never would.

"After my master's degree, I did a great deal of introspection. Although I did want a career in science, I also wanted a husband and children someday. But I knew if I stayed in school I would continue to be the same person I always was; I figured I would probably end up as a lonely professor in some university. I've known too many bitter female Ph.D.'s. I didn't want to be like them."

"So that's why you quit school and started working for me?"

"Right. I've frequently thought of quitting here and going back to school. If I'm going to be lonely, I might as well *have* the Ph.D. But I couldn't quit. I'm wrapped up in the experiment. I love those octopi as much as you do. And here I always . . . had the possibility of getting you to like me."

"I do like you, Sally. But I can't let myself like you . . . too much. It's . . . it's more than I said before. *I* was responsible for the breakup of my marriage; I'm a scientist, not a lover or a family man. I've never been particularly interested in people, and as a result I didn't know enough to be sensitive to my wife's feelings and moods. I'm not fit to be married to anybody . . ."

"Fred Solomon's a scientist and *he's* got a happy marriage."

"Fred's always been a friendly, gregarious person. I said before that he carried me out of some of the places we went to. He had to drag me to them in the first place. I'm sure a lot of scientists are like him. Maybe *I'm* the one who is different. But I know I can't be both a scientist and a person, too. I've tried it."

"You were lucky to have a friend like him to take you places. I never did. But, you see, that's the only thing that was different between us. We are, well, I think, meant for each other, Ray. I'm as naïve about people as you are—and we both know our problems now. We would be good for each other!"

"Look, Sally, I find you very attractive, perhaps too attractive. It's just that I can't. I'm—you are, too— we're both tangled up in spiderwebs from our past. I . . . can't do it again."

Sally stared at him with wide, tearful eyes.

"And here I am, using poetic imagery," Ray said. "Waiter! Could we have our check . . . ?"

When Ray walked a slightly drunk Sally from his air-car to the door of her condominium, she asked: "Would you like to come in for a little while to talk . . .?"

"No, Sally," he said coldly.

He was frustrated. He saw that his talk had had no effect, and turned and walked back to his car without saying good night.

"Hello, Ray! How's it going?" Fred asked as Ray Morgan slipped into his familiar seat in Otis's Restaurant.

"Fairly well," answered Ray, who didn't look as if he'd been doing well at all. He had bags under his bloodshot eyes, and his hair had more gray in it than ever. "I've been keeping busy, as usual. So your wife chased you out of the house again for a card game?"

Fred laughed. "That's a trumped-up charge. It's a deal we arranged so that she has time with her friends and I have time with mine."

Ray ignored the puns. "Well, if it works, good for you. I'm glad I could keep you busy while she has charge of the house."

"Yeah, thanks for coming. By the way, the other day, when I tried calling you at your lab to arrange this dinner, I spent a lot of time talking to Sally. I got the impression from her that you're overdoing the Save-the-alien-world-from-the-military idea."

"Why that little vixen!" Ray said, smiling. "That's just another one of her crazy schemes, uh, to get me to stop working so hard. I never figured she'd call in the infantry. Well, when it comes to my work, it won't do her any good, Fred. When I get involved in a project, I continue going until I drop or it's done, whichever comes first. You know that."

"Yes. I do. And you're right: Sally did ask me to get you to slow down. She told me the story of how you mistook the Atlantic Coast Train for the Miami Metro the other day, and ended up going five hundred kilometers when you only wanted to go five. But I managed to top her story by telling her about the time you tried studying in the bathtub and flooded out our whole apartment."

"Don't remind me of that, Fred."

"Sorry. But my point is, I don't care how hard you're working. I just don't want you working yourself to death for the wrong *reason*. I think you're hung up with fighting the military, when there's no reason to be."

"Okay, so what makes you think the military is so peaceful?"

"That's only a part of it. But let's order first. I'm starved. Margaret!"

Margaret had been walking near their table. She was busy tonight and hadn't noticed them come in, but she heard Fred's call and walked over. "Good evening, Dr. Morgan, Dr. Solomon. Would you like to order now?"

"Yes," Fred told her, "I'll have the filet mignon and a baked potato, and a salad with French dressing."

"And I'll have the usual, Margaret."

"I'll have your orders in a few minutes," she said as she finished punching the orders.

Once she had left, Fred said, "By the way, Sally was awfully concerned about your health, and about a lot of other things, too. Is something going on between you two?"

Ray frowned, then hesitated a few seconds. Finally, he smiled. "Keep your nose out of my personal life, dirty old man."

Fred grinned back. "What are you doing, getting crabby? You're into octopi, remember, not crustaceans."

After their dinner was served, Fred resumed the conversation. "You asked me what makes me think the military is so peaceful. Let me ask you what makes you think the aliens are so peaceful that we don't have to find out how to defend ourselves in case they decide to attack us. They might very well consider us invaders and decide they should attack. Why do you think they won't?"

"They aren't bug-eyed monsters, Fred. They're intelligent creatures with feelings like yours and mine. They're intelligent enough to know that killing is senseless unless it's absolutely necessary to survival. And besides, I've never said the aliens will be totally peaceful. I'm just complaining that the Navy plans to bombard the planet with H-bombs at the first action they interpret as hostile. And they can make any action *look* hostile."

"You have a paradox right there. You're saying the aliens won't try to kill us because they're as sentient as we are. But we'll kill them. If the fact that they're intelligent, feeling beings stops *them* from killing *us,* why doesn't it stop *us* from killing *them?*"

"I'm not saying they wouldn't try to kill us if they thought we were a threat to their existence, and if they thought it were possible. I just feel that some of those boobs in the military think the aliens are more of a threat than they are and therefore want to destroy them without real provocation. The aliens must be at least as peaceful as we are. They shouldn't be senselessly slaughtered."

"I don't think the aliens *are* as peaceful as we are . . ." Fred asserted. "And I have a number of good reasons. In the first place, if they're anything like our cephalopods, they're strictly carnivorous. They're hunters and killers by their very nature. And they don't have the option we have of growing our food from the soil."

"We can't assume that if they're carnivores they're murderers," Ray interrupted. "In fact, it may mean that they dislike senseless killing, since that would be wasting food."

"All right, I'll admit that I'm just speculating and that we can't be certain about intelligent carnivores. We've never encountered any before. But if you want to abandon speculation, then we also have to abandon any analogies about the aliens we draw from your experiments. In fact, all we really know about them is what we've observed from space: they have a fairly advanced technology and they are cephalopods."

"You know as well as I do, Fred, that we can trust the theory of convergence. The aliens are similar to our cephalopods because they developed in very similar environments. And those environments create animals which are very similar, no matter what their heritage. That's why the marsupial flying squirrels of Australia are almost identical to the normal mammalian flying squirrels of other lands. The *fleas* on both squirrels are all but impossible to tell apart!"

"All right, if we assume that convergence is a fact, and it probably is, I can use your octopi to show that the aliens don't have a reverence for life. Octopi are one of the few animals that fight to the death. And you, yourself, have said they've led you to believe that the aliens probably kill all but the best of their own children. If they will kill their own childen, how do you expect them to treat *us?* To them we're monsters from outer space. We can't expect them to have any reverence for our life if they don't even have reverence for their own."

"But that's their nature," Ray protested. "They're improving their own species. That proves they have a reverence for their species. To them, genetic breeding is probably like training a doctor is to us. It's a way of helping themselves."

"That may be, but it still shows that they have more respect for their species than they have for individual life. That's not good for us. If they happen to consider us dangerous to their survival as a species, they won't have any qualms about killing in order to protect themselves." .

"Well, I . . . don't—"

"How are things tonight, gentlemen?" Margaret asked when she had a few spare moments.

"Fine," Ray said, pleased with the interruption. "How are you, Margaret?"

"Busier than usual, but I'm doing all right on tips tonight. Oops, someone's calling. Enjoy your dinners."

The men continued their dinner in silence.

Finally, Fred asked, "Did you hear what happened to Ho-li Wong?"

"What? Did somebody finally shoot him?"

"No, he got promoted. He's now the Chief Administrator of the UN Science Foundation."

"Wong? He's an idiot. Why him?"

"I don't know. Somebody apparently thought he was doing a good job."

"Hell! There goes any hope I had for saving that planet. Wong and Admiral Vickman are buddy-buddy."

"That's not what *I* hear," Fred said. "They had a falling-out last month and are now at each other's throats. Wong's been pushing your soft line toward the aliens ever since."

Ray's face lit up. "That's a pleasant surprise! He may have a huge Napoleonic complex, but I need all the help I can get. I'll have to write him and congratulate him on his new job. Maybe we can work together toward creating friendly relations with Alpha Centauri Two."

"Writing him couldn't hurt."

"Oh?" said Ray. "Then you're with me on not destroying the aliens?"

"I never was *for* destroying your cephalopod world. I just feel that a lot of caution is necessary before we become too friendly with the natives."

"Some people can take that caution of yours and use it to *destroy* the natives."

"I doubt it."

"Let's get down to business," Ray suggested. "Have your people been making any progress in translating the aliens' radio transmissions?"

"None. It's completely different from any language we've ever worked with. We can't do anything without some clues to start us off."

"Tell me what you've got. I've been working on communicating with my octopi. Maybe I can help you."

"There's not much to tell. I can show you what we get on a display screen, or let you hear the narrow-band stuff; but to us it's all nonsense. We've been concentrating on two-dimensional picture transmission, thinking they probably communicate visually through a television-like system, but we don't get any sensible pictures."

"Octopi also can communicate through their sense of smell," Ray said. "Have you tried testing their signals that way: electrochemically?"

"No . . . but it might be worth trying."

Throughout the meal the two continued to discuss the aliens' methods of communication, and how to go about analyzing the signals the creatures were sending. While walking, alone, to the train station after dinner, Ray was thinking about how the octopi communicated by sight and smell, rather than with sound. He was wondering whether these differences would affect the way the aliens viewed abstract concepts and, therefore, affect their intelligence.

Lost in thought, he again forgot to switch cars on the Atlantic Coast Train and found himself in the wrong city.

"Let me show you one of my hologram tanks," Ray said to Ho-li Wong as they walked into one of three rooms which had a tank with a hologram setup in it.

"Fine."

"Sit here," Ray directed, leading Wong to one of the two computer consoles in the room. "Don't worry about touching any of the buttons. Your power's turned off."

Ray sat at the other console, turning it on as he got comfortable. He then switched the lights off in the room.

The tank was already lit. It had a dirt bottom with a few water plants scattered about. "Notice the far wall," Ray said. "There's a communications panel like the one I showed you before. But that isn't how we talk with the octopi here. We just use it t' teach them."

The buttons of this panel had no drawings on them. Above and below the panel the columns were numbered in red, and alongside the panel the rows were numbered in green.

"I see . . ." Wong said.

"Look at the coral wall on the left in the tank—that cave over there. D' you see those two octopus eyes?"

Two orange eyes containing vertical black pupils, and a big orange breathing funnel under the eyes, were all that could be seen of the octopus. It was sitting on the two arms that were folded underneath it. These arms were the color of the coral, so they could not readily be distinguished. The octopus's body and the rest of its arms were hidden in the cave.

"Is that its domicile?"

"Yeah. Now look at the glass box on the bottom of the other wall over there. That's my hologram display tank. It's set up t' give a full view 3-D image."

"Why, I perceive that the glass cube is a projection extending from another tank on the reverse of a partition. Is that an illusion which you have the machine portray whenever you're absent?"

"That's really super. You're right." Ray suddenly

stopped himself. He just realized that he had been slur-
ring his words, using more than his usual share of con-
tractions, and now he had used a needless exclamation.
"You've been doing that on purpose."

Wong smiled. He knew what Ray meant. "You are
referring to my language?"

"Yes. You do it to get a reaction out of people. Your
large words and structured speech got me subcon-
sciously to *un*structure my language as a reaction. You
do it on purpose to learn about people from their reactions—and to throw them off guard—don't you?"

"I am very impressed. Very few people realized what
I'm doing and why. And you are correct. My manner of
speaking is an affectation which I use for the reasons
that you've given. When I first entered politics, I decided
it would be useful and it has been. Whether people get
angered, or nervous, or change their own speech patterns, as you did, tells me a great deal."

"That's very interesting. Now that I know what
you're doing, I'll have to watch while you practice it on
somebody else."

"You're welcome to observe all you like. However, an
individual's responses when others are around are
usually different from what they are when I'm alone
with that person. But I'll be glad to discuss the reactions
with you afterward, if you desire. Incidentally, please
don't divulge the motivations behind my actions. My little secret wouldn't have much use if everyone knew my
motives."

"Sure. You can count on me." Ray realized he respected Wong and felt friendly toward him, now that
they were sharing a secret. Ray was also certain the
friendly feeling was mutual. "Let's get back to business.
As I was saying before, the image on the hologram is
there to make it look more natural to our octopi when
we put new images on the screen. Watch."

Ray typed a word on his keyboard and suddenly an
octopus came from the opening between the tanks, and
into the glass box. "That's my creation. I control him

with the console. I have a large number of programmed commands, each of which makes the image do different things. Right now, I have it acting happy and friendly. It's asking the real octopus to come out and play."

"I'm fascinated. Is this a product of *your* genius, Ray?"

Ray grinned. "Well, actually it's Sally's idea. But we both worked on it. Sally does the drawings, too. We take still holograms and feed them into the computer. Sally touches them up with a 3-D light pen to get our holos to say what we want them to. That's where Sally is now, working on some more drawings. Once she has finished a series of drawings, I have a computer program which animates them and reproduces them here."

"I see. She must be very talented."

"She is."

While Ray was talking, the octopus came out of its cave and crawled over to the hologram. Ray typed a succession of commands on his console, causing the image to move and change colors.

"The image I control is telling the octopus to go to the communications board and push the button six across, three up," Ray said. "If it does it correctly, it will get fed."

As soon as the imaginary octopus stopped giving directions, the real one swam to the panel in two rocket-like spurts and pressed the correct button. This caused a panel to open, releasing a school of small fish. The octopus began eating happily.

"I'm astounded. How did it ascertain precisely which button to push?"

"Octopi instinctively know a few 'words.' A mother octopus can tell her offspring to come to her, or go somewhere, by making a few color changes. We merely reproduce those color changes to get an octopus to come or go. Getting octopi to go to the right place is a little harder. A mother octopus will do it either by pointing, or by creating a picture of where she wants them to

go—on her interbrachial membrane. That's the skin between the arms.

"We originally had only one row of numbered buttons. We could tell an octopus to go, and then we'd
form, say, a '6' on the image's skin. It worked. The octopus went directly to the button with the '6' painted on
it. Using just a little bit of training, it wasn't hard to do
it with two numbers."

"Is their color-change mechanism actually capable of
reproducing numbers on their skin?"

"Yes, it's just muscles which cover chromatophore
cells. It requires the same type of muscle control of
them as lifting a finger does of us. The octopus has finished eating, so I'll demonstrate for you. Watch the part
of the interbrachial membrane under the eyes of the octopus once it starts giving signals."

Ray typed out another code word and the hologram
changed, such that the image of the octopus appeared to
be in a tank similar to the one containing the real octopus. Along one of the walls in the imaginary tank was a
communications panel similar to the one in the real
tank. Then Ray punched the button numbered "5, 9"
on the smaller panel near his desk, causing the button
of the same number-designation to light up in red in the
true octopus tank, but not in the imaginary tank.

The real octopus suddenly turned as red as the button. Then it began to change colors. As it did, the number "5" appeared in green and then the number "9"
appeared in red on the octopus's skin. The octopus kept
repeating these numbers until Ray typed out a few more
code words, causing the imaginary octopus to push button "5,9" on its panel. Then the real octopus crept back
to its cave, exhausted.

"That's an experiment I've been doing for a long
time with two real octopi," Ray said. "If one octopus
can't get the other to press the right button within two
minutes, both get shocks. Did you notice the small plastic square attached to the octopus's membrane in the

back?" Wong nodded. "That shocks the octopus when I press the right button. Just a mild shock. It doesn't do any damage, but it does cause a little pain."

"I am amazed that the octopus could reproduce numerals on its skin. You've progressed considerably since my previous inspection of your project."

"I have, but there's still a lot that has to be done. These octopi still aren't intelligent enough to handle a complex technological language, so I must continue with my eugenics experiments. I'll only keep the animals which pass the language down from one generation to another. And then I'll have to teach them to use tools and give them a scientific background. Also, I'll have to develop in them a sense of community and civilization. Then, lastly, I'll have to tell them who I am and why I've created them. Hopefully, teaching them won't be too hard, since I'll develop the language first. But it will still take some time."

"When do you surmise you will be able to terminate your experiments?"

"I think I might be able to do it in three years."

"Your timing is adequate. We hope to have obtained adequate translations of the aliens' communications by then. I judge that your results will assist us in formulating our decisions, once those translations are made."

"What do you think those decisions will be? Will we have peaceful relations with the aliens?"

"That is a function of the content of the translations. But at the current time, I perceive that most of those in positions of authority advocate belligerence toward the aliens—unless the translations prove them to be incredibly pacifistic. My recent altercation with Admiral Vickman stemmed from the belief that our decision should be made in an atmosphere of equanimity rather than in one of the predetermined fear."

"Then, you think most people want to destroy the alien world?" Ray asked, sounding naïve.

Wong smiled at Ray's question. "Well, they want to

argue from a position of force. But I'm out to moderate that position slightly."

"I'm with you," Ray said.

3

The mother octopus brought her children to the house of the sage. She had hoped that the sage would be outside his cave so he could talk to them, but all she was able to show them was the glass box he had built around his home. The sage was the only octopus to have ever used glass. No one could enter the sage's home and the sage never came out. One could talk to him only if he happened to be at the front of his cave, looking through the glass.

On this particular day the sage was not looking out, so the mother octopus could only tell her babies what *her* mother had told her. She told her children that the sage had always lived in this cave and always looked the same. He was a very old, small octopus, who never died. The sage knew everything that had ever happened to the community and everything that would happen to it in the future. Occasionally, the sage would come to the edge of his glass barricade and tell the octopi of disasters which were to occur.

Although the mother didn't know it, today was such a day.

The mother octopus decided to give up waiting for the sage to appear. She began crawling away from his home and called to her babies to follow her, but suddenly she smelled a call from one of them. She quickly turned around and saw the reason for her baby's alarm. The sage was at the front of his cave.

As soon as she had turned, the sage said, "Quick, get Longarms. I must talk to him." The sage saw her reluctance. He said, "Go. I'll take care of your babies. Go!"

The mother octopus could not disobey a command of the sage. She went to find Longarms, the leader of the community. The babies remained with the sage, who "talked" to them, testing their ability to communicate.

When the mother octopus returned with Longarms, the sage told her to take the children and go. Although she wanted to see what was about to be said, she obeyed the hologram.

"We are soon to be attacked by a creature that you've never before seen," the sage told Longarms. "It is big, longer than the span of your arms. And it has huge fins which make it look almost round from above. It is called an electric ray. It has a power which will kill, if the ray touches you with both its head and a fin at the same time. There is much you can learn from this power. I do not want this creature killed. I want you to capture it so that you can study its power."

"How are we to capture it?" Longarms asked the sage.

"Floating on top of our water are many sticks. Take these sticks and, with rocks, drive them into the ground. Make a large, circular cage from them. Once you've captured the electric ray, cover the cage with the large board which is also floating on our water. Use rocks to keep the board over the cage."

"How can we capture this monster if it has such power?"

"You can touch the ray if you keep a broad leaf between your suckers and the creature's skin. You may also touch its tail without harm. If you merely touch its fins or its head, you will receive a strong shock but will be unharmed. But if you are touched by both at the same time, you will die. If you work together with other strong males, each of you should be able to touch a part of the creature so that you can hold it still long enough to poison it. Your poison will not kill the ray. It will only stun it, so be careful."

"When will this electric ray come?" Longarms asked.

The sage did not answer. Instead, he retreated into his cave. Longarms was used to the way the sage behaved, and so did what the sage told him. He directed the other males to build the cage, and once it was done they arranged their plan of attack against the ray.

When the electric torpedo ray was released into the community tank the next day, the octopi were prepared. At the first sight of the creature, word of its arrival spread throughout the tank. The females and their offspring all disappeared into their homes, while the large males gathered around the sluggish monster.

The octopi anchored themselves to large rocks on the bottom of their tank as they waited for Longarm's signal to strike. Longarms waited as the huge ray, oblivious to the octopi, glided to the bottom. When the ray was within arm's reach of most of the octopi, Longarms gave the signal. In unison, each of the octopi shot forth an arm with which to grab one of the ray's two huge fins.

Some of the arms retreated as the surprised monster discharged its electricity. But most of the octopi suffered the electric shock and held on. The usually placid torpedo ray twisted and turned as it tried to escape, but the anchored octopi were too strong for it.

An octopus which had released its grip at the first electric shock again tried to get hold of the ray's pink fin, but this time the octopus was not firmly anchored to the ground. The ray pulled the octopus free from its moorings, carried it up to its head, and again released its charge. The octopus died instantly, though its suckers were still attached to the ray. The limp white body hung from the ray's fin.

Once the ray stopped fighting its captors, Longarms—with its tentacles wrapped in the broad leaves he had found in the tank—approached the head. Longarms brought his beak up to the monster's head and released his poison. Within seconds, the torpedo ray was limp.

The octopi quickly dragged the monster across the bottom of their tank, to where they had built the cage. As they did this, Longarms pried his dead comrade's suckers loose from the ray's fin. Longarms then carried the body of the dead octopus to an uninhabited corner of the large tank, from which it would mysteriously disappear by the next morning.

Meanwhile, the other male octopi put the unconscious torpedo ray into the cage they had built, and then put the cover on the cage, weighing the cover down with piles of large rocks.

Longarms went to the sage, who was at the glass barrier of his home, waiting for Longarms to come.

"I'm sorry about the death of your comrade," the sage said. "But that could not be prevented."

"He was young and foolish."

"Yes. You did a good job in capturing the electric ray. It will be a great help in your education. Now I want you to put a large fish in the cage with the ray. You should watch how the ray kills it with its 'electricity.' That is the name of the power. Then, using long sticks to hold various materials, touch the ray on both the head and fins with these materials. See the difference when you touch it with metal rocks and non-metal rocks. Then come back to me and I'll teach you about electricity, and show you how you can create it and use it to do work for you. Now, go. But come back tomorrow and you will learn."

The octopus did as he was told.

"You enjoy playing the wise old sage with those octopi, don't you?" Sally asked.

"Well, it's the best way to teach them," Ray explained. "I let them think they're learning from the mysterious old magician so their education will have a certain fascination to it. It helps them learn better."

"I think you're doing it because you enjoy it. You never leave that chair. You're looking at all those holovision sets of that big tank day and night."

"Well, if I'm going to be working all the time, I may as well enjoy it. And if I'm enjoying it, I'll be working more. It works both ways. There's nothing wrong with that. *You* did it with the drawings."

"Yeah, but you're still working too hard . . ." Then, after a pause, Sally asked, "When are you going to tell the octopi who you are and who they are? Have you decided yet?"

"Uh-huh. I figure that, once they have a firm understanding of electricity, they'll be able to grasp that their sage is really an image, and that the creator of that image also created their whole pattern of evolution."

"You mean you're going to tell them who they are as soon as you finish the electricity experiments?"

"I gather you don't think they'll be ready yet."

"Of course they won't be ready. You're going to tear down everything they know about themselves and their environment, and you expect them to just sit there and accept that destruction just because they've accepted electricity. It can't be done. You'll drive them all crazy."

"In the first place, I don't have much choice. I told Ho-li Wong I'd be done in the next three months, and I'm not going to let him down. And in the second place, the octopi are ready. I'm going to have the sage introduce *me* in his holographic box; then I'll replace this one-way glass, which we've been looking at them through, with two-way glass so they'll be able to see us. They'll have to believe they were developed by me, then. And they *are* ready to accept the idea. I know. I've given them their intelligence."

"They'll think it's all a creation of *their* magical sage. They're not ready to believe that *you're* the sage. They need a lot more experience with scientific concepts for them to think that they were created by science. It's ridiculous to try to tell them who they are. You'll just damage their sanity."

Ray was getting angry with Sally. He felt she was not only trying to dominate him, but also his experiment. In addition, his temper was being spurred by subconscious feelings of guilt that he was denying Sally her well-earned right to have some say in the experiment. Also in the back of his mind was the thought that perhaps she was right: that he *was* acting too quickly because of his commitment to Wong.

In anger, he said: "Look, Sally, you got your way with the holograms. You're not going to get your way now. This is my experiment and I'll do with it what I please. I'm not going to slow my progress because of your interference. I've had enough of that! Go back to your Octopus–English dictionary."

"I will! I don't care if your damned experiment collapses in your face at the last moment."

She stormed out of the room thinking that she should have quit a long time ago and gone back to school.

"Fred, hello," Ray said as his friend's face came into focus on the screen.

Fred's usually animated face looked tired and heavy. He had been up all night, though he looked as if he hadn't slept in a week.

"Did you complete the translation?" Ray asked him. "I've been dying to know what's been happening ever since you said their language was about to be cracked."

"Yeah, and it looks as if we've got trouble."

"Trouble? What kind of trouble? Are they warriors? Have we been completely wrong about them?"

"Well, they do sound rather aggressive. But it's worse than that: we've been discovered. They know we're in their solar system and that we're watching them. It's only been a few months since they first noticed us, but already they're talking about crash programs for building planetary defenses and constructing spaceships to meet us."

"That's just terrific," Ray said facetiously. "Now what are we going to do?"

"I don't know if they'll be followed, but the WSA has contingency plans for this type of situation. The aliens are behind us technologically, but we want to stop their military buildup. Therefore we should communicate with them as soon as possible. In addition, it will be to our advantage for the aliens not to suspect that we can eavesdrop on their broadcasts. Since they know we've been studying them, they probably wouldn't expect us to communicate with them until we've translated their language. Therefore, we'll have to make it seem as if we're forced to open communications between their world and ours. In other words, we'll have to purposely construct an accident whereby one of our devices crashes onto their planet, so that we'll appear to be forced to announce our presence to them."

"That sounds reasonable, but if you aren't going to use their language, how can we communicate with them?"

"That's the least of our problems. We'll use radio, at a frequency sure to attract their attention. And we'll send them lines of beeps, leaving some out here and there to make pictures. You know what I mean. It's an old idea—done all the time with x's and blanks on computer printouts. I've even got one. I'll send it to you over your repro. Be right back."

When Fred's picture was no longer on the holo-screen, Ray left his chair and went to the repro. He entered his code and extracted the printout. It contained the following pattern:

When Ray was once again seated at his holophone, Fred continued: "That's supposed to be a picture of a house, and the x's under it are our code for the word 'house.' With lines of beeps and blanks, we would expect any intelligent species to play with them until they get images which make sense. And once the aliens get the general system down, developing a whole language in code is easy."

"What kind of pictures would you send? The octopi wouldn't know that this is a house. You would need things that both species have in common, or you would just confuse them."

"Of course. We intend to start with pictures of things they'd recognize: diagrams of their stars, Alpha and Beta Centauri, as well as their system's planets, of the structure of hydrogen, and various concepts they'd probably be familiar with. But after sending those fairly simple images, we can send more and more complicated pictures until we have developed a full language. By computer it won't take too long."

"Now that you've told me how we're going to talk to them, what are we going to say?"

"Once they get the language down, we'll probably start by apologizing for accidentally crashing something on their planet. After that, the operation becomes more complicated. To lessen their suspicions of our eavesdropping, we'll tell them we've been in their system for less than a year. Also we'll say that we were keeping silent in order to assure ourselves that they were not belligerent. We'll tell them we're from Earth, but that—"

"Wait a minute. We're going to divulge our location to them? Are you sure our military people will let you do that? Isn't it dangerous in that they might come here and attack us?"

"In the first place, as I said before, the aliens are behind us technologically and at the moment they aren't much of a threat. Also, if they want our location very badly, they can build radio receivers sensitive enough to pick up the 'din' from our radar transmitters, radio beacons, non-directional ham radio transmitters, and similar VHF and UHF radiation. In the radio portion of the spectrum we must be the brightest thing in the sky of Alpha Centauri Two. And even if we were to try and stop such transmissions, our signals from four years ago would just be reaching Alpha Centauri now. But it's really no danger, since our distant location prevents a civilization which doesn't have both c-quantum energy and force-fields from doing *us* any harm. The force-fields cause the damage, or build bombs to cause the damage; and the faster-than-light energy brings the damage before any protection can be arranged. Although we have just begun translation, we are almost certain that the aliens have neither of these devices."

"Then we're safe. There's no reason at all to fear the aliens. We can go right ahead and start communicating with them."

"The situation is a lot more complicated than that. We may be safe *now,* but in order to remain safe we must make certain the aliens don't build force-fields and faster-than-light devices in the future. *Or* they might now have, or will build, something equally dangerous—something we've never even thought of. For those reasons, people like Admiral Vickman want to consider destroying the aliens at their first sign of belligerence, even though we've shown them to be technologically inferior."

"He's a bigger bastard than I thought."

"Maybe, but he does have a point. If we do as he says, we'll at least be safe."

"There's more to life than being safe, Fred."

"Of course there is. Don't argue with me. Go argue with Vickman. And besides, I don't have time to argue. I've got to get some sleep, so that I can get back to the translation project tomorrow. Good night, Ray."

"Wait a minute. You didn't say what we're going to tell the aliens in order to keep them from building force-fields and c-quantum devices."

"Oh, yeah. We'll tell them the devices we have in their solar system were brought there by a ship that took over twenty years to make the journey. We'll tell them the ship is still in their system but is hiding in the asteroid belt for the time being. Meanwhile, our machines and force-fields will begin building a mock-up of such a ship."

"Very good. That way, they won't even know we have force-fields and a faster-than-light communications device."

"That's right. I called you just to tell you what's happening, and I think that's everything. Now let me get some sleep. Good night, again, Ray."

"Good night."

Ray hung up the holophone. As he did, he realized this was the first time he could remember that Fred had talked to him without making even one pun.

"I've got some more bad news for you, Ray," Fred announced over the holophone, a few months later.

Fred looked well rested, but somewhat subdued. He seemed resigned to the fact that relations with the cephalopods were not going as well as he might have hoped.

"About the aliens? Have they responded to our message *already?* What did they have to say . . . ? What's wrong?"

"Mostly their attitude. But it's a lot of things. And you're right: it is amazing how fast they responded. Apparently their computers are as fast as ours. They deciphered the code messages almost as fast as we could send them."

"It seems as if you were wrong about the extent of their technology. They're not as far behind us as the WSA thought."

"No. It's more complicated than that. As I've been telling you for the past couple of months, they're behind us in some things and ahead of us in others. In physics, math, astronomy, and mechanics we are far ahead of them. In biology and in many of the social sciences, they are ahead of us. But it seems as if their computer technology is ahead of the rest of their mechanical technology."

"Enough about how fast they responded. What did they say?"

"They were very harsh, but amazingly honest. In essence, they accepted our apology for crashing an NMR spectroscope on their planet, but they said they don't trust us. They said they know we've been studying them for some time. They demanded that we end all spying upon their planet. They said they suspect that we have a faster-than-light communications device with which our ship, in their system, communicates with Earth. And they will not begin friendly relations with us until we show them our good faith by giving *them* such a device."

"That's all they said?"

"Yeah. We've been sending them more messages, but they refuse to respond."

"That doesn't sound very promising. Now what are we going to do?"

"I'm not really sure. Vickman and his followers want to threaten the aliens, to tell them we'll continue spying on them and will protect our spying devices if they try to stop them."

"That's awful. That can get us into a war."

"Right! And that's why Vickman's plan probably won't be used," Fred asserted. "I advocate that we explain c-quantum energy to the aliens, since that by itself can't pose any danger to us. Ho-li Wong supports me."

"Well, I hope you're right, and *your* plan is used. Do you think it would help make the aliens any more receptive if we had them talk to my octopi, rather than to humans? My animals are almost ready to talk to people on an intelligent level. We could tell the aliens there are two intelligent species on Earth, and perhaps they would like to talk to the one more like themselves in order to be convinced that we're kind to their fellow cephalopods."

"You know, that might work! It's worth a try, at

least. I don't know if the government will adopt the idea, but I'll bring it up and see what happens."

"Do you think if you got Wong working with you, you could arrange it? He's seen my octopi and he's impressed with them."

"It wouldn't hurt to bring him in. Wong's in a powerful position."

"Good. I'll call him and then call you back. All right, Fred?"

"Sure, Ray. You're our secret weapon. A sort of Ray-gun."

Ray said, "Good-bye," and hung up. He was smiling.

"Hello."

Ray looked up briefly. "Oh. Hi, Sally." He was busy typing at his computer console."

"What are you talking to them about today?"

"It's a class I started. Genetics," Ray said, without looking up from his typing.

Sally sat down at the other console and looked into the huge aquarium. "That's a big class you have. You must be a good teacher."

Twenty-three adult octopi were scattered around the hologram tank. In the space closest to the tank huddled three litters of young octopi, none of which was over four centimeters in height.

"If anything, my teaching probably sends them away. It's just that they have a great interest in learning, especially if it relates to how they were created."

Sally watched the hologram. Two figures were visible in it. One, the octopus sage, was lecturing about the structure of deoxyribonucleic acid. The other, a likeness of Ray Morgan, was using a blackboard. Ray's likeness was drawing the chemical representations of the DNA bases.

The students knew by then that the sage wasn't real, but that Ray needed it to communicate. Nonetheless, Ray kept his image in the hologram with the sage, to continually remind the octopi that *he* was the sage.

After a short while, Ray, still without glancing up, said to Sally: "I'm just about done with today's lesson. Would you like to say hello to my class?"

"Well, I . . ."

"Go on," Ray said, as he typed an introduction for Sally into his console.

The sage immediately responded by telling the octopi that Sally had just dropped in. Meanwhile, Ray's image pushed the blackboard out of the way.

Sally began typing at her console. In the hologram, an image of Sally appeared where the blackboard had been. Next to her image was the image of a female octopus.

"Hello," Sally's octopus said. "How do you like Ray's lessons? Is he a good teacher?"

Most of the adult octopi had pictures on their skin saying that they approved of Ray's teaching. The majority of the children, however, were communicating with each other. Some of them were laughing about Sally's appearance.

Sally saw them. She had her octopus say, "I don't want to keep you. If Ray has no objections, your class is over. You may do as you wish." Sally then caused the hologram screen to go blank, and the octopi dispersed.

"Why didn't you talk to them some more, Sally?" Ray asked. "They won't bite."

"Yeah, I know. But they saw I had nothing to say to them."

"It's good for them to talk to someone besides me. And you're the only other person who knows their language." Ray paused, but Sally said nothing. Finally, he added, "Well, never mind. I've got to write programs for more of their lessons and I need your help on some of the drawings. Let's get started."

They concentrated for about twenty minutes, until Sally asked, "Why are you still working so hard, Ray? Our octopi have done everything we've wanted them to. And until the government makes a decision about them, we don't know what to prepare for. Why don't you take a break or a vacation or something?"

She had been depressed lately, both because her work at the lab constricted her social life, offering her none even with Ray, and because she felt the experiment was not really hers. She released some of her frustration by badgering Ray. In addition, she hoped that he appreciated her display of concern for him, rationalizing that outwardly he might become angry but inwardly he might like her better because she cared.

Ray was merely annoyed. He assumed that her efforts were intended to impress him and therefore were, to a great extent, phony. However, he tried not to show his annoyance.

"I can't do that," he answered. "I've got these lessons I want to teach. If my octopi talk to the aliens, or to other people here on Earth, I want them to be well educated. And there's still the breeding experiments we've got going in the other tanks. Plus, there's a great deal I can learn from just talking to the octopi."

"I can take over your lessons for you, if you want. And the other experiments aren't really so necessary anymore, now that we've got *these* octopi. You've been working twenty hours a day for the past five years. Your hair's turning gray, and your eyes are always bloodshot. You need a rest. And this is the first time you can really take it. Nothing's pressing anymore, at least not for a while."

"Now look, Sally, you and Fred have been trying to get me to slow down for—what did you say it was— five years? And it still hasn't done you any good." Ray was starting to get angry.

"But now's the first time you can really rest. A couple of days off is just what you need."

She was trying to be calm and yet determined, hoping that by doing so Ray might respect her point of view and finally relax. She was also thinking that if he took some time off, he might spend some of it with her. Or, as consolation, he would leave her in charge of the lab.

"Just stop it. I don't want to talk about my needing a rest anymore."

"I was just concerned for your health. But if you want to kill yourself, that's not my problem."

"Will you stop mothering me!"

"I'm not mothering you," Sally said quietly. "I just think you need a rest. You look and act awful, because you're always overtired."

"Don't tell me what I need!" Ray was frustrated by Sally's calm persistence. "Just because you're an old maid doesn't mean you have to adopt me as a husband. I don't want you as a wife."

Sally was now struggling with herself. Her body was trembling but she managed to keep her voice even. "I'm not acting," she lied. "I'm just concerned that—"

Ray slapped her.

Not hard. He *had* intended to hit her hard, but he caught himself almost in time. He slapped her lightly across the face.

Her first reaction was one of anger. Who are you to do something like that? she thought, but stopped herself from saying it out loud. As she checked herself from yelling, she realized that she shouldn't blame Ray. It was *her* fault. She had wanted to show concern, but instead had made him angry. She began to cry.

Also running through Sally's mind were other thoughts, of which she was only dimly aware—more mature ideas, cold, logical, and utilitarian. Sally was partly conscious that perhaps Ray's hitting her would be of some benefit. She reasoned that he would suddenly feel sorry and be sympathetic, now that he no longer felt so superior.

Ray was shocked. It was the first time he had hit anyone since a boyhood fight he had in junior high school. All his anger faded and was replaced by confusion and concern.

"I'm sorry, Sally. I . . . I don't know what got into me. I didn't mean to do that."

He came over to her and put his arm around her

shoulder. Then, with his handkerchief, he started dabbing at the tears running down her cheeks.

Sally looked up at him with tear-filled eyes. Suddenly, he felt more tender toward her than he had felt for anyone in his life.

He kissed her, and it became a long, passionate kiss.

Finally, he pulled away, confused. He had discovered feelings for Sally which were far deeper than those he had ever felt for his wife; but still he was angry with himself for having them. Until that moment he had been in control of his relationship with Sally. He had known that he cared for her, but was master of his emotions and could keep their relationship businesslike. But now he was no longer in command of the situation, and he was afraid. He felt that his soul was severing itself from his rational mind.

"I shouldn't have done that," he said, more to himself than to Sally.

"But . . . you are glad you did?"

"Yes."

Ray paused. He wanted to be with her, but he also wanted to be alone with his thoughts. He decided on the latter course. "Are you all right?" he asked.

"I'm fine." Outwardly, Sally appeared calm, even slightly cold toward Ray. But tears were still streaming down her cheeks.

"Let's quit for the day."

"All right."

"Alone, I mean. I just want to be able to think about things. You don't mind, do you?"

"No." She began smiling faintly, sure of Ray's emotions now.

Ray was less sure about both his and Sally's feelings. "And you'll be back tomorrow?"

"Of course."

"Good night . . ."

Ray knew he sounded awkward. He put his hands on her shoulders, wanting to kiss her again, but stopped himself. Instead, he smiled at her, then hesitantly turned and started down the lawn, back to his house.

On his way, Ray thought about everything that had happened. He was in a dreamlike state. Mechanically, he went into his bedroom and lay down on the bed. For so long he had kept from having an emotional relationship, for fear it would dominate his life. Now he found he loved Sally and knew he was no longer in control of himself.

He started crying, but his tears were more for joy than for sadness.

When Ray awakened early the next morning, he found himself in pajamas. He must have changed sometime in the middle of the night, but he did not remember awakening. Remaining in bed, he began to straighten out his thoughts. Then, after a while, he got dressed and walked to the building housing his octopi. When he got to the room with the large hologram tank, he found Sally already there.

Stopping a few meters from her, he said: "Sally, I . . . I love you. I've been fighting myself for so long that I couldn't recognize it until I was hit with it."

Sally smiled. "You're forgiven: for everything."

When their kiss ended, Ray continued talking, realizing he was babbling but knowing he had to tell her all his feelings.

"I can't imagine how I could ever hit you. I would rather die first. But I'm glad I did it: I mean I needed it—a slap in the face, *my* face. And hitting you provided it. But our lives together won't be spent playing, like my other time. I mean we'll spend our time here, working. These octopi are as much your life as they are mine. And we'll be together a lot, though most of it will be here. You don't mind, do you?"

"Of course not." And she kissed him again.

Ray found himself playing with the buttons on the back of Sally's blouse. Realizing what Ray was doing, she began kicking off her shoes, but Ray stopped her.

"Let's make one exception," he said. "There's one thing we'll do together that we won't do here. I'll race you to the bed in *my* house!"

They both started running.

Sally, running her hardest, giggled the whole way. Ray paced himself so as not to outdistance her. The combination of the cool morning ocean breeze and the hot Florida sun felt good on Ray's face. The sight of Sally, her long hair blowing behind her and the white sand kicked up by her bare feet, made Ray's body tingle with excitement. He was happier than he had ever been in his life.

They were still in bed a while later when Ray brought up the subject of his octopi. "Last night did something else for me—other than bringing us together."

"Oh. What?"

"Before last night, I had thought the aliens would be friendly and peaceful, like my . . . *our* octopi."

"And now you don't?"

"No. I figured that any intelligent beings would be beyond using violence, at least with other intelligent beings. But after what *I* did last night, I did a lot of thinking about violence and I don't think intelligence has much to do with it anymore."

"Why's that?"

"Well, I might be rationalizing my own action, but I think violence is more of an instinctive thing. We can't help ourselves. It's in our genes. And it is probably in the genes of the alien creatures. Fred told me they sounded aggressive from their own radio broadcasts, and he was probably right."

"But I thought you said the way we translated the messages made them sound aggressive. You also said the aliens wouldn't be aggressive since our own octopi aren't."

"Our octopi don't have any meanness in them because I didn't breed for it. An underlying assumption of our experiment is that similar animals developing in similar environments would be analogous, both mentally and physically—like the convergence of the Australian and American flying squirrels. But the one difference in the environments of the aliens and our octopi is that *we are interfering*. Perhaps unconsciously, I've inflicted my own prejudices upon the breeding of our octopi, whereas the aliens have probably developed naturally. My prejudices lean toward removing aggressiveness from my octopi, so I've tended to breed innate meanness out of them. But the aliens would have instinctive aggressiveness because it would help their species to survive. Fighting among themselves would have helped intensify the natural selection processes, and therefore help their species improve itself."

"So you think we shouldn't make friendly overtures to the aliens? They might someday attack us?"

"I don't know if I want to make a judgment like that, but I am going to call Fred Solomon and Ho-li Wong and talk it over with them and give them the benefit of my new opinions."

Sally grinned. "Do you realize we're lying in bed together, talking about octopi and aliens?"

"I know," Ray said. He began laughing. "Let's remedy that situation."

He put his arms around her and made love to her once more.

"But Fred, you should do something," Ray said into his holophone. "I called Wong and he was nice about it, but he thinks I'm crazy. You're the only one left. If you and the WSA want to, we can slow this thing down."

"You're the one who proposed the idea. Now that the aliens have finally responded and have agreed to talk to your octopi as a prelude to friendly communication with us, you can't stop it. It's the one break we needed to start peaceful relations."

"But I don't know if we *should* have peaceful relations. This thing should be thought out slowly and carefully. If we act friendly to them without thinking, they might eventually destroy us."

"Everything *has been* thought out slowly and carefully, Ray. What do you think the WSA, the Navy, and a great many other organizations have been doing for the past twelve years? And besides, we've translated many of the aliens' radio communications for these twelve years and know a good deal about them."

"All right, here are a couple of things I recently thought of—thanks to my new outlook—that you probably haven't considered. Suppose the aliens conduct genetic breeding on their *own* children. You saw what I did in ten years. If the aliens are what I think they are, they've been doing it for centuries. They're probably much better at genetic breeding than I am. They can breed supermen in no time."

"Supercephalopods. Let's call them supercephs, for short."

"Don't joke about it. It's true. With their super . . . uh . . . superbeings, their technology will develop a lot faster than ours. And although they might now be behind us technologically, they may *think* better than we do. Their pictographic language handles broader concepts more easily than our word language. It's easier for them to conceive abstract ideas. With their language and their superbeings, they'd surpass us in no time, and then in order to insure their own safety, they'd destroy us."

"You're not telling me anything we haven't already thought about, Ray."

"Huh?" Ray looked shocked.

"We exobiologists at WSA have been reading your reports for the past twelve years, Ray—and not only your reports. We've also had access to the Navy's, and to a lot of others'. One of my colleagues has been saying for years that the aliens evolve faster than we do. He suspected the aliens of conducting their own genetic breeding. Now that we've translated their radio communications, we've confirmed that the aliens do evolve faster—

for that very reason. But we know about it and we can plan keeping that in mind."

"If we know about it, how do we make use of our knowledge of them to keep the aliens from surpassing us technologically?"

"That's not hard. We're still technologically superior, and the aliens know that. They'll approach us for technological information and we'll supply it. But we'll only supply what we *want* to supply. Anything we don't want them to have, we can tell them we don't have; and that it's impossible to make. So, by giving them little hints of things, we can get them interested in certain fields of research. In other words, we can see to it that their research money, and brilliance, gets channeled wherever we want it to go.

"For example," Fred continued, "the aliens suspect we have a faster-than-light method of communication, but that's all they suspect. We'll tell them we sent our machines into their system in a sub-light-speed, interstellar robot ship, so they'll have no suspicion that we have force-fields which build things in their system. If they knew of our force-fields, they might insist we give them one; and if we refused, they would put a great deal of effort into developing one of their own. But since they don't know we have force-fields, they won't ask for them, and with a few discreet statements on our part the aliens won't even do any research into creating them."

"But what about the c-quantum transmitter? I thought we weren't going to give that to them."

"Now that we got the aliens to agree to talk to us without giving them anything, I think we'll give them the transmitter anyway, as a measure of good faith. That is, we'll give it to them assuming their conversation with your octopi turns out all right!"

"But isn't it dangerous to give it to them? You've said that the faster-than-light device is one of the two things which could make the aliens dangerous to us."

"Yeah. But by itself the transmitter isn't dangerous.

I, and the rest of us at WSA, think we should give the aliens the communicator because it actually *decreases* the chance of danger. The fact of our giving something important to them increases their trust in us. And that trust can be used to discourage them from developing force-fields. Also, if we didn't give it to them, they would probably put a great deal of effort into creating one, anyway. Their study of faster-than-light forces might open whole new branches of their physics, as it did for us, so that they would also develop many other things—some of which might be dangerous."

"So you hope to stunt their development of science by handing things to them on a silver platter?"

"I don't like the idea of inhibiting science, either; but to protect our own safety, that's what we'll have to do. As a matter of fact, instead of telling them how to *make* a c-quantum device, we plan on *giving* them one. It'll be an in-space transfer between our fake interstellar ship and one of their new ships. It's a nice gesture to give them something of ours and it tells them how to make one of their own.

"Incidentally, Ray, we at first wanted to fake the octopi–alien communications by using your holograms instead of the real octopi. But the aliens insisted on a smell transmission device in addition to a 2-D viewer. Since the aliens don't have holography, we can't use 3-D. We felt we couldn't fake the scent transmission, so we'll have to use real octopi."

"That's good. I'd rather do it with the real octopi, anyway. And we can trust them, Fred. My octopi won't do anything wrong. They use their smell the same way we use facial expressions. It won't cause any problems . . ."

Ray had been fidgeting in his chair for some time while he and Fred were talking. Now, he hesitantly brought up the subject that was bothering him. "Fred, I've realized that there are an awful lot of things you haven't been telling me, things that might have benefited me to know for my experiments."

"What things?"

Fred was smiling faintly. It was a nervous type of smile, but it also displayed some of Fred's amusement at his friend's method of broaching a potentially touchy subject.

"You said a colleague of yours knew about the aliens' rate of progress, and that you suspected their high intelligence. Why didn't you ever tell me about those things."

"Both ideas were just speculation, and I never really believed the faster rate of progress idea. But it was more than that. You and I are good friends. The same thing which gives me the right to ask how you and Sally are getting along gives me the right to censor some of the information I give you, if I feel that information will damage you in some way, especially if the information is only speculation."

"I'm not sure I agree with that. I don't know if even a good friend knows enough about a person to judge what sort of things won't be good for him. But never mind that. Why did you feel those ideas weren't good for me?"

"I thought you might work better if you didn't know that the aliens were so far advanced that they had done everything you were doing long before you did it. I thought you'd find it depressing to believe you were doing something novel and find out it wasn't so novel. And with the idea that the aliens *think* better than we do, I didn't want you to feel you had to create supermen, or rather," Fred laughed, "supercephs. I didn't want your goal to be too difficult, so that you had to create something *more* brilliant than you—we—are. I know my reasons don't sound very convincing; but in light of the fact that what I was keeping from you were just idle suspicions, I think they're valid."

"Perhaps. But why didn't you tell me about your plans to control the aliens' technology? *Those* weren't just idle speculations."

"Until we knew for certain that the aliens *were* technologically inferior, those were just contingency plans. We had the same sort of plans if the aliens were our equals or superiors. If we told them all to you, you wouldn't have felt compelled to work so hard in order to save the aliens from the military."

"In other words, you were using me to get more work done."

"In a sense, you can say that. We were using your personal fantasies. We were also using Admiral Vickman's desire for war—to get him to work harder. Telling him some of our plans might have prevented him from getting the military to spend so much on cephalopod research. But it's all the same as Ho-li Wong using his fondness for long words for his purposes, or my using my enjoyment of puns for my purposes. In this case, the foibles of many people went into realizing a desired goal: friendly relations with the intelligent aliens of Alpha Centauri Two."

"I'm your friend, and didn't even suspect you. I should have known."

"Well, cephalopods are always using their suckers. Can we help it if they found you to be an extra one?"

Ray groaned.

As the picture of the alien appeared on the two-dimensional television screen, the audience gasped. The alien looked more like a squid than an octopus. It had twelve arms, each containing hundreds of suction disks. In addition to the arms, the creature possessed two long and winding tentacles. Just beyond the junction of the arms and tentacles were two bulging eyes with round pupils. There was also a large black funnel, through which the alien breathed. Surrounding the eyes and funnel was the thick mantle, which bulged out around the alien's brain and then tapered off into a sleek body. The body had circular fins on either side.

Although Ray considered both octopi and squid to be

beautiful creatures, he felt revulsion at the sight of the alien. To Ray, the alien resembled a very deformed squid, and he considered the deformities ugly.

When it first appeared, the alien had a uniformly faint pink color. Now its head region began to change color. It was speaking.

Ray translated for the audience of important dignitaries, and for the rest of the world, which was watching the holovision broadcast of the event.

"Greetings." As Ray translated the first word, all whispering by the audience ceased. "Our reception is quite good. We see you very clearly."

Ray was surprised at how well the alien had learned his octopus language from the dictionary Sally had made. He had no trouble translating.

Sally, in turn, translated for the octopi. Three octopi were in the tank with the television, Spider, Phantom, and Longarms. Although Longarms was still fairly young, as octopi go, he was no longer the most advanced octopus, having been superseded by the younger generation. Nevertheless, Ray let Longarms talk to the aliens, since he was quite experienced in dealing with the unknown. All three octopi had been well briefed on what to say. They were in a special tank with a scent-transmitting device and a two-dimensional screen. In addition, there were several hologram cameras in the tank, since all the world was watching on holovision.

"Hello," Longarms said. "We are receiving you quite well also."

"Good," the alien replied. "We wish to talk to you, before getting into serious communication with the humans of Earth, in order to allay the fears of our people. We are cautious beings and we felt that, since the Earthlings are so alien to us, their sight might frighten the people of our planet. We felt that communicating first with the cephalopods of Earth might alleviate those fears. We want it known that we mean to offend neither the humans nor yourselves.

"We do not wish to put you in an awkward situation

by asking you questions about matters the Earth people might find sensitive. We will try to keep our questions as harmless as possible. First, if you will, we would like you to describe the Earth's intelligent land beings and their environment. Since our planet has little land and no land creatures, we are very curious about them."

The octopi began telling what they had seen or had been told or had been told to say about humans. Then they had a chance to ask questions of the aliens. Ray found the translations of these unrehearsed answers more difficult than the earlier translations, but he managed to translate, nevertheless.

After about three hours, the communications ended on friendly terms.

"I'm glad that's over!" Sally told Ray, once everyone else had left and the three octopi were returned to their tank. "What did you think of it?"

"Rather than talk about it here, let's see what the octopi think. After all, they're the ones who did the actual communicating with the aliens."

"All right."

Ray and Sally sat down at their computer consoles outside the tank. They had developed a system whereby they talked through the hologram box, not only with the octopi but also between themselves. So as not to exclude the octopi from their conversations, Ray and Sally did not talk out loud. Instead, they typed their messages into the computer, which reproduced their typing as messages on the skin of the fake octopi in the hologram box. Since both Ray and Sally knew their octopus language, perfectly, they could communicate in this manner quite easily, and the octopi could listen in and join the conversation.

The octopus named Spider began the conversation. Among Longarms, Spider, and Phantom, Spider was the smallest. However, he had very bright eyes and was the most dynamic of the three. He asked, "Well, what did you two think of the whole thing? Did we do a good job?"

"A *very* good job! We had no complaints. I don't even think Admiral Vickman had any complaints," Sally replied.

Sally and Spider had a fondness for each other. Ray, however, preferred Longarms to Spider.

"That surprises me," Spider said. "And what did you think of the aliens?"

Ray continued to let Sally talk. "I was impressed. I thought the aliens were very polite. They seemed peaceful, and I was amazed at how well they learned our language."

Ray finally joined in the conversation. "The language they had down pretty well. But peaceful? I don't think so."

"Why not?" Sally asked. "They seemed friendly enough. They didn't ask the octopi any *bad* questions."

"It's like I told the newscasters. The reason the aliens asked all those questions about humans is that they will probably try to breed intelligent primates the way I bred intelligent cephalopods."

"I thought they don't know we were bred by you," Phantom said. "You told us the aliens thought we developed naturally."

"They do, or at least we *think* they do. But those alien squid have been applying the principles of genetic breeding for centuries. Their techniques of genetic breeding and genetic engineering are probably much better than ours. They'll have to breed men from fish, whereas I bred intelligent cephalopods from nonintelligent cephalopods. But they're so much more advanced than we are in the area of genetic engineering that it probably won't take them more than a few centuries."

"I agree with Ray," Longarms said. "Their plan for genetic breeding of humans must be the reason for all their questions. And besides, I received a faint sense of a deceitful purpose from their scent."

"I smelled it, too," Phantom added.

"All right. Then what does that bode for the future?" Spider asked.

"At the moment, I think we're safe," Ray replied, "since our technology is better than theirs and we have some control over the way their technology develops. But over the next few centuries they'll be studying the creatures they develop, in order to learn more about us. The more they learn about us, the less control we'll have over them. Eventually, I think they'll pass us technologically, and then they may destroy us to secure their own safety."

"*No!*" Spider's skin had turned slightly red with anger. "I completely disagree. I admit the aliens are trying to learn more about us in order to decrease our control over them. But they will not destroy us. I received that from their scent."

"I agree with Spider," Longarms said calmly. "I imagine that over the next few hundred years there will be a great deal of tension between Alpha Centauri and Earth, but I am certain there will be no war. After a while there will develop a trade, of sorts, between the two worlds. Then will come an intermingling of cultures. Eventually, though they are very different, the two cultures will begin to develop as one civilization. It will take a great deal of time, and it will occur as the two species explore the galaxy together. But there will be peace."

"I agree with Longarms," Phantom said. "I smelled no *war* in the alien's scent."

"I also agree with Longarms," Sally said. "Unfortunately I don't have the octopi's sense of smell, but what Longarms said sounds logical."

Ray paused for a few seconds, thinking about Longarms speech. Finally he said, "It does sound probable, and it likely will happen that way. At least, I hope it does."

Spider changed the subject of the conversation. "Ray, what's going to happen to us? Are we free to go explore your world? Do we coexist with humans, as equals? Or are we, as your creations, subservient to you and to other humans?"

"As far as I'm concerned, you may do as you wish, though I would like you, or at least some of you, to stay here and help me with my experiments. At the moment, however, you are very valuable to the government in helping to understand and communicate with the aliens, so I don't know if I would be allowed to let you go free.

"In fact, due to our different environments, it would cost a great deal to arrange for you to travel around the Earth on land. Even if we released you into the ocean, to protect you and our investment in you we would have to supply you with communication and protection devices. These things cost money—money you would have to get from the government."

"So we're stuck here?"

"Not necessarily. If you cooperate with the government over the next few weeks, I may be able to get Fred, or Ho-li Wong, to help me in securing you the money from the government. I'm sure that in gratitude for what you've done for us, the government would be willing to assist you in taking trips around the world and such. You'll probably be big celebrities."

"Thank you. We'd appreciate it if you looked into it for us," Phantom said.

"Sure. I'd be happy to."

"We have one more request of the two of you," said Spider.

"Yes?"

"Would it be possible for you to give us control of the computers outside our tanks?"

"Of course. But why do you want it?" Sally asked.

"So we could take over some of the responsibilities of running this place."

"But I still don't know why you want it."

"Well, we were hoping that you could give us complete responsibility for this station, so the two of you would be free to go off on a honeymoon together."

Ray glanced at Sally. They both smiled, and in unison said aloud, "Let's do it."

Between the third and fourth planets of the star Alpha Centauri is a belt of asteroids, small planets, and planet-like bodies which are usually composed of iron or silicon, but which occasionally may be ice or frozen gases. Due to the great number of them, a fairly large object could hide among the asteroids and remain unnoticed by any intelligent beings within the star system.

In the year 2077 over a thousand man-made objects were hidden in this asteroid belt. The objects included enough bombs to destroy a world. Also included were scanning devices which were able to study the tiniest disturbances that occurred on the second planet of the Alpha Centauri system. The asteroid belt also contained an unmanned spaceship, which had been designed to look as if it had crossed four light-years. The ship, however, had been built within the asteroid belt.

On the twelfth of February, this spaceship came out of hiding. Using ion-propulsion rockets, it traveled to the second planet of the star system, taking thirty-seven days to get there.

As the unmanned "interstellar" ship approached the second planet, a ship left the planet to greet the visitor. Both ships achieved orbit around the planet. The orbits coincided, and finally the two ships were just ten meters apart.

Under the control of Earthmen more than four light-years away, the dummy interstellar ship slowly opened a hatch to the outside and a long arm appeared telescoping outward until its tip was four meters beyond the ship. Attached to the tip was a small metal canister containing a device identical to the one which the ship itself used to communicate with the Earthmen.

Suddenly a small explosion occurred at the end of the arm, releasing the container. The canister spun, as it slowly moved away from the interstellar ship. The ship now fired its rockets to park it in a permanent orbit around the alien world.

The other spaceship also fired its rockets, but it moved in pursuit of the container ejected from the first ship. As it approached the container, the front of the spaceship opened to form two gaping jaws with which it could grab the device from Earth. The ship was responding to signals from its planet: the intelligent beings of Alpha Centauri's second planet did not yet have faith enough in their technology to entrust themselves to it in space.

The alien spaceship maneuvered itself until the container thrown from the other ship was within the gaping jaws, and the jaws began to close. Although the insides of these mechanical mandibles were padded with very soft material to protect the valuable device, their closing was like the biting off of a piece of foreign technology which the beings of the planet would digest and use with, and against, their new neighbors.

The alien spaceship returned home to its planet, its valuable prey safely guarded within its jaws. ☆